NIGHTSHADE AND DAMNATIONS

GERALD KERSH was born in Teddington-on-Thames, near London, in 1911. He left school and took on a series of jobs—salesman, baker, fish-and-chips cook, nightclub bouncer, freelance newspaper reporter—and at the same time was writing his first two novels. His career began inauspiciously with the release of his first novel, *Jews Without Jehovah*, published when Kersh was 23: the book was withdrawn after only 80 copies were sold when Kersh's relatives brought a libel suit against him and his publisher. He gained notice with his third novel, *Night and the City* (1938) and for the next thirty years published numerous novels and short story collections, including the novel *Fowlers End* (1957), which some critics, including Harlan Ellison, believe to be his best.

Kersh fought in the Second World War as a member of the Coldstream Guards before being discharged in 1943 after having both his legs broken in a bombing raid. He traveled widely before moving to the United States and becoming an American citizen, because "the Welfare State and confiscatory taxation make it impossible to work over there, if you're a writer."

Kersh was a larger than life figure, a big, heavy-set man with piercing black eyes and a fierce black beard, which led him to describe himself proudly as "villainous-looking." His obituary recounts some of his eccentricities, such as tearing telephone books in two, uncapping beer bottles with his fingernails, bending dimes with his teeth, and ordering strange meals, like "anchovies and figs doused in brandy" for breakfast. Kersh lived the last several years of his life in the mountain community of Cragsmoor, in New York, and died at age 57 in 1968 of cancer of the throat.

HARLAN ELLISON (b. 1934) is a prolific American writer best known for his short stories and screenplays in the science fiction genre. In over fifty years of writing, he has created over seventy books, ten screenplays, numerous television scripts, and seventeen hundred short stories. The *Washington Post* called him "one of the greatest living American short story writers," and the *Los Angeles Times* proclaimed him the "20th Century Lewis Carroll." He has won the Hugo Award nine times, the Nebula Award four times, the Bram Stoker Award five times, including its lifetime achievement award, the Edgar Award twice, and the World Fantasy Award twice, among many other awards. He lives in California.

By Gerald Kersh

Novels

Jews Without Jehovah
Men Are So Ardent
Night and the City
The Nine Lives of Bill Nelson
They Die with Their Boots Clean
Brain and Ten Fingers
The Dead Look On
Faces in a Dusty Picture
The Weak and the Strong
An Ape, a Dog and a Serpent
Sergeant Nelson of the Guards
The Song of the Flea
The Thousand Deaths of Mr. Small
The Brazen Bull
Prelude to a Certain Midnight
The Great Wash
Fowlers End
The Implacable Hunter
A Long Cool Day in Hell
The Angel and the Cuckoo
Brock

Story Collections

I Got References
The Horrible Dummy and Other Stories
Clean, Bright and Slightly Oiled
Neither Man nor Dog: Short Stories
Sad Road to the Sea
Clock Without Hands
The Brighton Monster and Other Stories
Guttersnipe
Men Without Bones
On an Odd Note
The Ugly Face of Love and Other Stories
More Than Once Upon a Time
The Hospitality of Miss Tolliver
Nightshade and Damnations

NIGHTSHADE AND DAMNATIONS

GERALD KERSH

With an introduction by
HARLAN ELLISON

VALANCOURT BOOKS
Kansas City, Missouri
2013

Nightshade and Damnations by Gerald Kersh
Originally published Greenwich, Conn.: Fawcett, 1968
First Valancourt Books edition 2013

Published by Valancourt Books, Kansas City, Missouri
Publisher & Editor: James D. Jenkins
20th Century Series Editor: Simon Stern, University of Toronto
http://www.valancourtbooks.com

Library of Congress Cataloging-in-Publication Data

Kersh, Gerald, 1911-1968.
 [Short stories. Selections]
 Nightshade and damnations / Gerald Kersh ; introduction
by Harlan Ellison. – First Valancourt Books edition.
     pages cm
 ISBN 978-1-939140-15-9 (acid free paper)
 1. Short stories, American. 2. Horror tales, American.
 3. Science fiction, American. I. Title.
 PR6021.E743N55 2013
 823'.912–dc23

                          2013003252

All Valancourt Books publications are printed on acid free paper
that meets all ANSI standards for archival quality paper.

Set in Dante MT 11/14

INTRODUCTION

Kersh, the Demon Prince

NIGHTMARES, phantasmagoria, horrors that lurk in the streets of today, the corrupting weaknesses of men; these are the bones and gristle of what this book contains.

The flesh is the talent of Gerald Kersh.

In England, Kersh is a much-revered author. His books are seldom out of print. They honor and respect him. Which is a bit unusual, when one considers that Kersh is an American, and that here in America we barely know his work. In ugly point of fact, his brilliant novels *Night and the City* and *A Long Cool Day in Hell* cannot be obtained, and the very best of his works, *Fowler's End*, has never been reprinted.

It gives one pause. Why should it be so? Almost any hack who can write in something that approximates the English language can get published these days. Lady novelists unfit to carry Kersh's pencil box sell millions in paperback. Non-novelists who rearrange the facts of contemporary history in narrative form find themselves lionized. Rock singers mislabeled poets scatter the pearls of their illiteracy across the bookstalls and get lotta pieces green paper in return. Then why should it be true that a man who has been captivating audiences with his offbeat and penetrating stories for over a quarter of a century should find it close to impossible to reach a wide American audience . . . ?

I'll be nice today. I won't castigate the American reading public. It is too often led to the literary slaughter for me to kick it in the rump while it waits for the butcher's hook. I'll offer instead a totally specious reason for Kersh's unfamiliarity to most readers, and thereby work into a rationale for this book having been edited by a man who has never met Gerald Kersh.

Burn your newspaper!
Shut your door and slip the police latch!

Sit with lights out in a darkness that deepens!

Now . . .

Now you begin to live in the dark night of the soul.

And in that endless night you meet Kersh.

Kersh, damn him, the Demon Prince. Who speaks thus:

> "We hang about the necks of our tomorrows like hungry harlots about the necks of penniless sailors."

Kersh, who can describe the indescribable:

> "A man has a shape; a crowd has no shape and no color. The massed faces of a hundred thousand men make one blank pallor; their clothes add up to a shadow; they have no words. This man might have been one hundred-thousandth part of the featureless whiteness, the dull grayness, and the toneless murmuring of a docile multitude. He was something less than nondescript—he was blurred, without identity, like a smudged fingerprint. His suit was of some dim shade between brown and gray. His shirt had gray-blue stripes, his tie was patterned with dots like confetti trodden into the dust, and his oddment of limp brownish mustache resembled a cigarette-butt, disintegrating shred by shred in a tea-saucer."

Damn thee, Kersh, bastard! How many times have I tried to describe such a man and crumbled the paper into my waste basket? How many times have I sought the images, and never found them? Damn you, Kersh, for showing me, and all of us who strive to capture magic in a shot glass, how much better you are, how much more easily you can do it! For someone who has never tried to write, it looks simple. But like all great art—like the dancing of Fred Astaire and the silken sculpture of Calder—its complexity is best expressed by its appearance of simplicity.

No, I've never met Kersh. But I'm editing Kersh, because it takes one to know one.

It takes somebody who writes about households filled with

LSD hippies who turn into vampires to know somebody who writes about a man who is pursued by men without bones. It takes somebody who writes of the soul of a hooker trapped in a slot machine to know somebody who writes of the man who found the Lid to the Under World. It takes somebody who knows the face of nightmare to truly introduce somebody who deals in night-shade and damnations.

As you may have gathered, I admire Gerald Kersh and his work almost shamelessly. His stories have intrigued and stimulated me for many years. When I was asked to put together this marvelous group of stories, I considered it a rare privilege and honor.

Then I set about reading everything I've ever read by Kersh, not to mention half-a-hundred others that had slipped past me somehow. From those stories I've selected what I consider to be the very finest, most memorable pieces Kersh's endlessly inventive mind has let escape.

But in the selection, oh what serendipity! what side benefits! what extra treasures I found:

A phrase of such penetrating rationality, that I had it printed on big yellow cards, which I give to my friends, that reads:

> ". . . there are men whom one hates until a certain moment when one sees, through a chink in their armor, the writhing of something nailed down and in torment."

A random chance phrase that captured my imagination wholly; stopped me, stunned, at the perfection of the imagery:

> "A storm broke, and at every clap of thunder the whole black sky splintered like a window struck by a bullet—starred and cracked in ten thousand directions letting in flashes of dazzling light, so that I was stunned and bewildered."

A special character, who lumbered or flopped or hurled himself across the pages of a story so unforgettably that he became a real person, someone added to my list of authentic acquaintances.

But it is not merely for the terror and strangeness and breath-holding qualities that I commend these Kersh fables to you. Each of them says something potent and immediate about the world in which we live.

Depending on how you want your mind bent, "Whatever Happened to Corporal Cuckoo?" once and for all demolishes the myth of military nobility . . . or solidifies it for all time.

"The Queen of Pig Island" says something new and terrible about the nature of love. "The Ape and the Mystery" indicates a rational size for the cap-A in Art. "A Lucky Day for the Boar" might well be printed as a small pamphlet and included in any orientation kit given to young executives starting in at advertising agencies. "Voices in the Dust of Annan" and "The Brighton Monster" comment with a kind of hideous clarity on war and where it leads us.

And I've included "Busto Is a Ghost, Too Mean to Give Us a Fright!" because of the sheer unexcelled brilliance of the descriptions therein. There are others, as well, that make salient points about what is happening to you today . . . but mostly they're here because they are whopping good yarns.

Kersh still writes, and better than ever, I'd venture. But he isn't a bright-eyed, bushy-quilled writer of twenty any longer. As Kersh is so painfully persistent in reminding us, we all die. But most men die, and no one knows they have passed this way. It can never be so with Kersh. He is leaving a legacy—expanding with each impact of a typewriter key—that has influenced, and is still influencing, generations of younger writers.

By the excellence of what he has done, Gerald Kersh infuriates and spurs other writers to try and beat him at his own game.

Perhaps one day, one of us will realize that it is impossible to beat a Demon Prince. The sonofabitch uses magic. No mortal can write this well.

HARLAN ELLISON
New York City

September 5, 1967

NIGHTSHADE AND DAMNATIONS

CONTENTS

THE QUEEN OF PIG ISLAND

THE story of the Baroness von Wagner, that came to its sordid and bloody end after she, with certain others, had tried to make an earthly paradise on a desert island, was so fantastic that if it had not first been published as news, even the editors of the sensational crime-magazines would have thought twice before publishing it.

Yet the von Wagner Case is commonplace, considered in relation to the Case of the Skeletons on Porcosito, or "Pig Island," as it is commonly called.

The bones in themselves are component parts of a nightmare. Their history, as it was found, written on mutilated paper in Lalouette's waterproof grouch-bag, is such that no one has yet dared to print it, although it happens to be true.

In case you are unacquainted with the old slang of the road: a grouch-bag is a little pouch that used to hang about the necks of circus performers. It held their savings, and was tied with a gathered string, like the old-fashioned Dorothy-bag. This was necessary, because circus-encampments used to be hotbeds of petty larceny. So, on the high trapeze, the double-back-somersault man wore his grouch-bag. The lion-tamer in the cage of the big cats might forget his whip or lose his nerve—he would never forget or lose his grouch-bag, out of which could be filched the little moist roll of paper-money that was all he had to show for his constantly imperiled life.

Lalouette carried her grouch-bag long after the gulls had picked her clean. It contained 6,700 dollars and a wad of paper with a scribbled story, which I propose to make public here.

It is at once the most terrible and the most pathetic story I have ever had to tell.

At first the captain of the ship who landed on Porcosito, who subscribed to a popular science magazine, thought he had discovered the missing link—the creature that was neither man nor ape. The first skeleton he found had a sub-human appearance. The thorax was capacious enough to contain a small barrel; the arms were remarkably long, and the legs little and crooked. The bones of the hands, the feet, and the jaw, were prodigiously strong and thick. But then, not far away—it is only a little island—in a clump of bushes, he found another skeleton, of a man who, when he was alive, could not have been more than two feet tall.

There were other bones: bones of pigs, birds, and fishes; and also the scattered bones of another man who must have been no taller than the other little man. These bones were smashed to pieces and strewn over an area of several square yards. Wildly excited, happy as a schoolboy reading a mystery story, the captain (his name was Oxford) went deeper, into the more sheltered part of Porcosito, where a high hump or rock rises in the form of a hog's back and shelters a little hollow place from the wind that blows off the sea. There he found the ruins of a crude hut.

The roof, which must have been made of grass, or light canes, had disappeared. The birds had come in and pecked clean the white bones of a woman. Most of her hair was still there, caught in a crack into which the wind had blown it or the draft had pulled it. It was long and fair hair. The leather grouch-bag, which had hung about her neck, was lying on the floor in the region of the lower vertebræ, which were scattered like thrown dice. This human skeleton had no arms and no legs. Captain Oxford had the four sets of bones packed into separate boxes, and wrote in his log a minute account of his exploration of the tiny island of Porcosito. He believed that he had discovered something unexplainable.

He was disappointed.

The underwriters of Lloyd's in London had, with their usual punctiliousness, paid the many thousands of pounds for which the steamship *Anna Maria* had been insured, after she went down near Pig Island, as sailors called the place. The *Anna Maria* had gone down with all hands in a hurricane. The captain, officers, passengers, cargo, and crew had been written off as lost. Faragut's Circus was on board, traveling to Mexico.

Captain Oxford had not found the remains of an unclassified species of overgrown, undergrown, and limbless monsters. He had found the bones of *Gargantua the Horror, Tick and Tack, the Tiny Twins,* and *Lalouette.*

She had been born without arms and legs, and she was the queen of Pig Island. It was Lalouette who wrote the story I am telling now.

Tick and Tack were tiny, but they were not twins.

A casual observer sees only the littleness of midgets, so that they all look alike. Tick was born in England, and his real name was Greaves. Tack, who was born in Dijon, Brittany, was the son of a poor innkeeper named Kerouaille. They were about twenty-five inches tall, but well-formed, and remarkably agile, so that they made an attractive dancing-team. They were newcomers to the circus, and I never saw them.

But I have seen Gargantua and Lalouette; and so have hundreds of my readers. *Gargantua the Horror* has haunted many women's dreams. He was, indeed, half as strong and twice as ugly as a gorilla. A gorilla is not ugly according to the gorilla standard of beauty; Gargantua was ugly by any reckoning. He did not look like a man, and he did not quite resemble an ape. He was afflicted by that curious disease of the pituitary gland which the endocrinologists term *acromegaly.* There is a well-known wrestler who has it. Something goes wrong with one of the glands of internal secretion, so that the growth of the bones runs out of control. It can happen to anyone. It could happen to me, or to you; and it produces a really terrifying ugliness. Gargantua, as it happened, was by nature a man of terrible strength; George Walsh has told me that he might have been heavy-weight weight-lifting champion of the world. An astute promoter realized that there was money in his hideousness; so Percy Robinson rechristened himself. *Gargantua the Horror* grew a beard—which came out in tufts like paint-brushes all over his face—and became a wrestler. As a wrestler he was too sweet-natured and silly, so he drifted into a sideshow. Naked to the waist, wearing only a bearskin loincloth, he performed frightening feats of strength. In a fair in Italy I saw him lift on his back a platform upon which a fat man sat playing a grand piano. That same evening I saw Lalouette.

I would not have seen her if I had not been in the company of a beautiful and capricious woman who said, when I told her I had a prejudice against going to stare at freaks, that if I would not come with her she would go in alone. So I bought the tickets and we went into the booth.

Lalouette was an aristocrat among freaks. She drew great crowds. Having been born without arms and legs she had cultivated her lips and teeth, and the muscles of her neck, back and stomach, so that she could dress herself, wash herself, and, holding a brush or pencil in her lips, paint a pretty little picture in watercolors or write a letter in clear round longhand. They called her Lalouette because she could sing like a bird. One had the impression that she could do anything but comb her hair. She could even move a little, by throwing her weight forward and sideways in a strange rolling motion. Lalouette painted a little picture while we watched, and sang a little song, and my lady friend and I, overcome with admiration and with pity, agreed that a woman of her accomplishments might have been one of the greatest women in Europe if the Lord in His wisdom had seen fit to make her whole. For she was a lady, superbly educated, and extremely beautiful—a blonde with great black eyes and magnificent hair of white-gold. But there she was, a freak on a turntable; nothing but a body and a head, weighing fifty pounds.

I had some conversation with her: she spoke five languages with perfect fluency, and had read many books. Enquiring into her history I learned that she came of a noble, ancient, overbred Viennese family. Indeed, royal blood ran in her veins, and some fortuneteller had told her mother the Countess that the child to which she was about to give birth would be a ruler, a queen.

But when the child was born they saw a monstrosity. The Count fainted. The Countess loved Lalouette and cherished her, devoted her wretched life to the unfortunate girl, who, soon after she could speak, demonstrated a proud and unyielding spirit. Conscious of her infirmity, Lalouette wanted to do things for herself, despising assistance—despising herself.

Her father could not bring himself to look at her. When she was seventeen years old her mother died and her father sent her away with her nurse. "All the money that you need, take," he said, "only do not let me see this abortion." Then, when the First World War came, the Count lost all his money and shot himself. The kind old nurse lost much of her kindness after that, and when an agent named Geefler offered her money if she could persuade the girl to go with him, the nurse, pleading sickness and poverty, had no difficulty in persuading Lalouette that this would be a good thing to do.

So the young lady changed her name. Geefler sold her to Gargamelov, who passed her on to Faragut; and she drew money up and down the world, until Faragut's Circus went towards Mexico, and the *Anna Maria* was wrecked, and she found herself with *Tick and Tack* and *Gargantua the Horror* on Porcosito, the island of pigs.

Then the prophecy came to pass. She was the queen of Pig Island. She had three subjects: two dancing dwarfs and the ugliest and strongest man in the world; and she had no arms and no legs; and she was beautiful.

Gargantua was a man whose tenderness was in inverse proportion to his frightful ugliness. As soon as the *Anna Maria* began to sink he went instinctively to the weakest of his friends and offered them his muscles. To Tick and Tack he said: "Hold on to my shoulders." They were in sight of land. He took Lalouette in his left hand, told the others to hold tight, and jumped overboard, and swam with his legs and his right hand. The ship went down. The Horror swam steadily. He must have covered five miles in the face of a falling high wind. At last his feet touched ground and he staggered up to a sandy beach as the sun was rising. The two little men were clinging to him still. His left hand, stronger than the iron which it could bend, held Lalouette. The dwarfs dropped off like gorged leeches, and the giant threw himself down and went to sleep—but not before he had made a hollow place in the soft, fine sand, and put Lalouette comfortably to rest.

It was then, I believe, that Gargantua fell in love with Lalouette. I have seen it happen myself—in less outrageous circumstances, thank God! The strong makes itself the slave of the weak. And he saved her life. It is the tendency of man to love that which he has risked his life to save.

Unhappy Gargantua! Poor Horror!

Armless and legless, Lalouette was the brain. In spite of her disability, she was the queen of Pig Island. She was without hope and devoid of fear; so she could command, since everything was clear in her mind. And she had read many books. Lalouette said: "Tick and Tack; there must be water here. One of you go to the left. The other goes to the right. Look for the place where things grow greenest——"

"Who d'you think you are, giving orders?" said Tick.

She said: "Oh yes, and another thing; empty your pockets."

Tick had, among other things, a leather-covered loose-leafed notebook. Tack had a remarkably large-bladed knife which he carried, no doubt, to give himself confidence; but he was a fierce little man at heart. They all had money. Gargantua had a fine gold cigarette-lighter, and a few hundred sodden dollars in a sea-soaked pocket—he alone wore no grouch-bag. Lalouette had strung about her neck with her grouch-bag, a gold pencil.

"We'll need all these things," she said.

"Who the hell d'you think you are, giving us orders?" said Tick.

"Be quiet," said Gargantua.

Lalouette continued, "That lighter is of no use as a lighter, because it's full of water. But it has flint and steel! It strikes a spark. Good. Gargantua, leave it to dry."

"Yes'm."

"You two, on your way right and left, had better pick up dry drift-wood—the drier the better. We can strike a spark with that lighter and make a fire. Having lit a fire we can keep it burning. It must not ever be allowed to go out. Your knife, Tack, will be useful too. . . .

You, Gargantua, will go up the beach. There is a lot of wood here from ships. So there must be iron. Wood from ships has always iron. Iron is always useful. In any case bring wood that has been cut. We will build a little house. You shall built it, Gargantua—and you too, Tick, and you also, Tack. I shall tell you how you must build it."

Tick began to protest. "Who d'you think——"

"Leave the lighter so that it dries in the sun," said Lalouette, "and take care that your knife is dry and clean, Tack."

"Always," said Tack.

Gargantua said: "Here's my lighter; you can have it if you like— it's solid gold. A lady gave me it in France. She said——"

"You can have my notebook if you like," said Tick sullenly. "It's solid leather, that cover. Pull that gadget down and those rings open and the pages come out."

"Please, if you will allow me, I will keep my knife," said Tack.

"You may keep your knife," said Lalouette. "But remember that we may all need it, your knife."

"Naturally, Mademoiselle Lalouette."

"Who does she think——" began Tick.

"*Shush!*" said Gargantua.

"No offence, Lalouette," said Tick.

"Go now, please. Go!"

They went. Tick found a spring of fresh water. Tack reported the presence of wild pigs. Gargantua returned with an armful of wreckage; wood spiked with rusty nails; a massive thing like a broken mast in which was embedded an enormous iron pin.

"Light the fire," said Lalouette. "You, Gargantua, make a spear of that long piece of iron. Make it sharp with stones. Then tie it tight to a stick. So you can kill pigs. You and you, Tick and Tack, go up to the rocks. I have seen birds coming down. Where there are birds there are eggs. You are light, you are dancers. Find eggs. Better still, find birds. When they sit on their eggs they are reluctant to go far away from their nests. Approach calmly and quietly, lie still, and then take them quickly. Do you understand?"

"Beautifully," said Tack.

Tick said nothing.

"Better get that fire going first of all," said Gargantua.

Lalouette said: "True. Boats must pass and they will see the smoke. Good, light the fire."

"If I could find another bit of iron, or something heavy," said Gargantua, "I could do better than this spiky sort of thing, Miss. I dare say I could bang it out to a bit of a blade once I got the fire going good and hot."

"How?" said Lalouette.

"I was 'prentice to a blacksmith, 'm," said Gargantua. "My dad was a smith, before the motor-cars came in."

"What? You have skill then, in those great hands of yours?"

"Yes'm. Not much. A bit, but not much."

"Then make your 'bit of a blade,' Gargantua."

"Thank you, 'm."

"Can you make me a comb?"

"Why, I dare say, yes. Yes, I should say I *could* make you a bit of a comb, 'm. But nothing fancy," said Gargantua, shutting one eye and calculating. "Something out of a little bit of wood, like."

"Do so, then."

"Yes'm. If Mr. Tack doesn't mind me using his knife."

"Could you also build a house, Gargantua?"

"No 'm, not a house; but I dare say I might put you up a bit of a shed, like. Better be near the drinking water, though. And I shouldn't be surprised if there was all sorts of bits of string along the beach. Where there's sea there's fish. And don't you worry— I'll bring you home a nice pig, only let me get that fire going nice and bright. And as for fish," said Gargantua, plucking a nail out of a plank and making a hook of it between a finger and thumb— "sharpen that up and there you are."

"Clever!" said Tick, with malice.

"But he always was clever," said Tack tonelessly, but with a bitter little smile. "We already know."

Gargantua blinked, while Lalouette said, "Be quiet, please, both of you."

Then Gargantua nodded and growled, "That's right. You be quiet."

Tick and Tack exchanged glances and said nothing until Lalouette cried: "Come! To work!"—when Tick muttered, "Who the
hell do they think they are, giving orders?"

"Come on now, you two!" shouted Gargantua.

I believe it was then that the two midgets Tick and Tack began
to plot and conspire against Gargantua the Horror, and I am
convinced that they too in their dwarfish way were in love with
Lalouette.

They followed Lalouette's instructions, and struck sparks out
of Gargantua's lighter to kindle powdery flakes of dry driftwood
whittled with Tack's big-bladed knife. Tick blew the smolder into
flame and the men fed the fire until it blazed red-hot, so that Gargantua, having found a thick slab and a pear-shaped lump of hard
rock for his anvil and hammer, beat his iron spike into a good
spearhead which he lashed to a long, strong pole. Then they had a
crude but effective pike, with which Gargantua killed wild pigs.

Porcosito is not called Pig Island without reason. It used to be
overrun with swine, bred from a pedigree boar and some sows
that Sir John Page sent to Mexico in 1893, in the *Ponce de Leon*,
which was wrecked in a squall. Only the pigs swam ashore from
that shipwreck. Porcosito seems to be an unlucky island.

Gargantua hunted ruthlessly. The pigs were apathetic. The
boars charged—to meet the spear. The four freaks ate well. Tick
and Tack fished and caught birds, gathered eggs and crabs. Lalouette directed everything and at night, by the fire, told them stories
and sang to them, recited all the poetry she could remember,
and dug out of her memory all she had read of philosophy.
I believe that they were happy then; but it makes an odd picture—the truncated beauty, the stunted dancers, and the ugliest
man on earth, grouped about a flickering fire while the songs of
Schubert echo from the rocks and the sea says *hush . . . hush . . .*
on the beach. I can see the sharp, keen faces of the midgets; and
the craggy forehead of the giant wrinkled in anguish as he tries to
understand the inner significance of great thoughts expressed in
noble words. She told them stories, too, of the heroes of ancient
Greece and Rome—of Regulus, who went back to Carthage to

die; of the glorious dead at Thermopylæ, and of the wise and cunning Ulysses, the subtlest of the Greeks, who strove with gods and
came home triumphant at last. She told them of the triumph of
Ulysses over Circe, the sorceress who turned men into beasts; and
how he escaped with his crew from the cave of the one-eyed giant
Cyclops. He was colossal; the men were small. Ulysses drilled his
sailors to move like one man, and, with a sharpened stick, blinded
the giant and escaped.

She let them comb her hair. The French dwarf Tack was skillful at this, and amusing in conversational accompaniment to the
crackling of the hair and the fire. Tick hated his partner for this.
Yet the gigantic hands of Gargantua were lighter on her head than
the hands of Tick or Tack—almost certainly because the little men
wanted to prove that they were strong, and the giant wanted to
demonstrate that he was gentle.

It was Gargantua who combed Lalouette's beautiful bright hair,
evening after evening, while Tick and Tack sat exchanging looks.
No words: only looks.

Sometimes the little men went hunting with Gargantua. Alone,
neither Tick nor Tack could handle the heavy spear. But it must
be remembered that they were a dancing team, trained to move
together in perfect accord. So, while Tick directed the forepart
of the shaft, Tack worked close behind him, and they put their
combined, perfectly synchronized strength and agility into a dangerous leap-and-lunge. Once they killed a fat boar. This must have
made them confident of their power to kill.

This is not all guesswork. I have ground for my assumption, in
what Lalouette wrote in Tick's loose-leaf notebook, holding the
gold pencil in her teeth and guiding it with her lips, before she
bit the paper into a ball and pushed it with her tongue into her
grouch-bag.

It takes courage and determination to kill a wild boar with
a spear. A boar is fearless, powerful, unbelievably ferocious,
and armored with hard hide and thick muscle. He is wickedly
obstinate—a slashing fury, a ripping terror—two sickles on a bat-
tering-ram, animated by a will to kill, uninhibited by fear of death.

Having killed a boar, Tick and Tack, in their pride, resolved to kill Gargantua.

Lalouette says that she, unwittingly, gave them the idea, when she told them the story of Ulysses and Cyclops.

But the foolish giant called Gargantua the Horror, billed as the strongest and ugliest man on earth, must have been easy to kill. He worked all day. When Lalouette's hair was combed and her singing ceased, he went away modestly to sleep in the bushes. One night, after he had retired, Tick and Tack followed him. Gargantua always carried the spear. Lalouette listened drowsily for the comforting rumble of Gargantua's snoring a few yards away; she loved him, in a sisterly way.

. . . *Ha-khaaa . . . kha-ha . . . khaaaa-huk . . . khaaaa . . .*

As she listened, smiling, the snoring stopped with a gasp. Then Tick and Tack came back carrying the spear, and in the firelight Lalouette could see that the blade of the spear was no longer clean. The redness of it was not a reflected redness.

Thus she knew what the little men had done to Gargantua. She would have wept if she could; but there was no hand to wipe away her tears, and she was a proud woman. So she forced herself to pretend to be asleep.

Later she wrote: *I knew that this was the end. I was sorry. In this place I have felt strangely calm and free, happier than I have ever been since my dear mother used to hold me in her arms and tell me all the stories I told here; stories of gods and heroes and pygmies and giants, and of men with wings . . .*

But that night, looking through the lashes of her half-closed eyes, she saw Tick untying the blade of the spear. He worked for an hour before he got it loose, and then he had a sort of dirk, more than a foot long, which he concealed in a trouser-leg. Tack, she thought, had been watching him also; for as soon as Tick closed his eyes and began to breathe evenly, he took out the knife which he had never allowed them to take away from him, and stabbed his partner through the heart.

He carried the body out of the range of her vision, and left it where he let it fall—Lalouette never knew where.

Next morning Tack said to her, "At last we are alone. You are my queen."

"The fire?" she said, calmly.

"Ah yes. The fire. I will put wood on the fire, and then perhaps we may be alone after all this time."

Tack went away and Lalouette waited. He did not return. The disposition of his bones, and the scars on them, indicate that he was killed by a boar. There was no more driftwood nearby. Tack went into the trees to pick up whatever he might find. As I visualize it, he stooped to gather sticks, and looked up into the furious and bloody eyes of a great angry boar gathering itself for a charge. This must be so; there is no other way of accounting for the scattering of his shattered bones. Hence, the last thing Tack saw must have been the bristly head of a pig, a pair of curled tusks, and two little red eyes. . . .

The last words in what may be described as Lalouette's journal are as follows:

A wind is blowing. The fire is dying. God grant that my end may be soon.

This is the history of the Queen of Pig Island, and of the bones Captain Oxford found.

FROZEN BEAUTY

Do I believe this story?

I don't know. I heard it from a Russian doctor of medicine. He swears that there are certain facets of the case which—wildly unbelievable though it sounds—have given him many midnight hours of thought that led nowhere.

"It is impossible," he said, "in the light of scientific knowledge. But that is still a very uncertain light. We know little of life and death and the something we call the Soul. Even of sleep we know nothing.

"I am tired of thinking about this mad story. It happened in the Belt of Eternal Frost.

"The Belt of Eternal Frost is in Siberia.

"It has been cold, desperately cold, since the beginning of things . . . a freak of climate.

"Did you know that a good deal of the world's ivory comes from there? Mammoth ivory—the tusks of prehistoric hairy elephants ten thousand years dead.

"Sometimes men digging there unearth bodies of mammoths in a perfect state of preservation, fresh enough to eat after a hundred centuries in the everlasting refrigerator of the frost.

"Only recently, just before Hitler's invasion, Soviet scientists found, under the snow, a stable complete with horses—standing frozen stiff—horses of a forgotten tribe that perished there in the days of the mammoths.

"There were people there before the dawn of history; but the snow swallowed them. This much science knows. But as for what I am going to tell you, only God knows. . . ."

I have no space to describe how the good doctor, in 1919, got lost in the Belt of Eternal Frost. Out of favor with the Bolsheviks, he made a crazy journey across Siberia toward Canada. In a kind of sheltered valley in that hideous hell of ice, he found a hut.

"... I knocked. A man came; shabby and wild as a bear, but a blond Russian. He let me in. The hut was full of smoke, and hung with traps and the pelts of fur animals.

"On the stove—one sleeps on the brick stove in the Siberian winter—lay a woman, very still. I have never seen a face quite like hers. It was bronze-tinted, and comely, broad and strong. I could not define the racial type of that face. On the cheeks were things that looked like blue tattoo marks, and there were rings in her ears.

"'Is she asleep?' I asked, and my host replied; 'Yes; forever.' 'I am a doctor,' I said; and he answered; 'You are too late.'

"The man betrayed no emotion. Maybe he was mad, with the loneliness of the place? Soon he told me the woman's story. Absolutely simply, he dropped his brief sentences. Here is what he said:

I have lived here all my life. I think I am fifty. I do not like people around me.

About fifteen ... no, sixteen years ago I made a long journey. I was hunting wolves, to sell their skins. I went very far, seven days' journey. Then there was a storm. I was lucky. I found a big rock, and hid behind it from the wind. I waited all night. Dawn came. I got ready to go.

Then I see something.

The wind and storm have torn up the ground in one place, and I think I see wood. I kick it. I hit it with my ax. It is wood. It breaks. There is a hole.

I make a torch and drop it down. There is no poisonous air. The torch burns. I take my lamp and, with a little prayer, I drop down.

There is a very long hut. It is very cold and dry. I see in the light of my lamp that there are horses. They are all standing there frozen; one with hay or something, perhaps moss, between his teeth. On the floor is a rat, frozen stiff in the act of running. Some great cold must have hit that place all of a sudden—some strange thing, like the cold that suddenly kills elephants that are under the snow forever.

I go on, I am a brave man. But this place makes me afraid.

Next to the stable is a room. There are five men in the room. They have been eating some meat with their hands. But the cold that came stopped them, and they sit—one with his hand nearly in his mouth; another with a knife made of bronze. It must have been a quick, sudden cold, like the Angel of Death passing. On the floor are two dogs, also frozen.

In the next room there is nothing but a heap of furs on the floor, and sitting upon the heap of furs is a little girl, maybe ten years old. She was crying, ever so long ago. There are two round little pieces of ice on her cheeks, and in her hands a doll made of a bone and a piece of old fur. With this she was playing when the Death Cold struck.

I wanted more light. There was a burned stone which was a place for a fire.

I look. I think that in the place where the horses are, there will be fodder. True; there is a kind of brown dried moss. The air is dry in that place! But cold!

I take some of this moss to the stone, and put it there and set light to it. It burns up bright, but with a strong smell. It burns hot. The light comes right through the big hut, for there are no real walls between the rooms.

I look about me. There is nothing worth taking away. Only there is an ax made of bronze. I take that. Also a knife, made of bronze too; not well made, but I put it in my belt.

Back to the room with the furs in it, where the fire is blazing bright. I feel the furs. They are not good enough to take away. There is one fur I have never seen, a sort of gray bear skin, very coarse. The men at the table, I think, must have been once, long ago, strong men and good hunters. They are big—bigger than you or me—with shoulders like Tartar wrestlers. But they cannot move any more.

I stand there and make ready to go. There is something in this place I do not like. It is too strange for me. I know that if there are elephants under the frost, still fresh, then why not people? But elephants are only animals. People, well, people are people.

But as I am turning, ready to go, I see something that makes my heart flutter like a bird in a snare. I am looking, I do not know why, at the little girl.

There is something that makes me sorry to see her all alone there in that room, with no woman to see to her.

All the light and the heat of the fire is on her, and I think I see her open her eyes! But is it the fire that flickers? Her eyes open wider. I am afraid, and run. Then I pause. *If she is alive?* I think. *But no*, I say, *it is the heat that makes her thaw.*

All the same, I go back and look again. I am, perhaps, seeing dreams. But her face moves a little. I take her in my arms, though I am very afraid, and I climb with her out of that place. Not too soon. As I leave, I see the ground bend and fall in. The heat has loosened the ice that held it all together—that hut.

With the little girl under my coat, I go away.

No, I was not dreaming. It is true.

I do not know how. She moves. She is alive. She cries. I give her food; she eats.

That is her, over there, master. She was like my daughter. I taught her to talk, to sew, to cook—everything.

For thousands and thousands of years, you say, she has lain frozen under that snow—and that this is not possible. Perhaps it was a special sort of cold that came. Who knows? One thing I know. I found her down there and took her away. For fifteen years she has been with me—no, sixteen years.

Master, I love her. There is nothing else in the world that I love. She has grown up with me, but now she has returned to sleep.

"That's all," the doctor said.

"No doubt the man was mad. I went away an hour later. Yet I swear—her face was like no face I have ever seen, and I have traveled. Some creatures can live, in a state of suspended animation, frozen for years. No, no, no, it's quite impossible! Yet, somehow, in my heart I believe it!"

THE BRIGHTON MONSTER

I FOUND one of the most remarkable stories of the century—a story related to the most terrible event in the history of mankind—in a heap of rubbish in the corridor outside the office of Mr. Harry Ainsworth, editor of the *People*, in 1943.

Every house in London, in those dark, exciting days, was being combed for salvage, particularly scrap metal and waste paper. Out of Mr. Ainsworth's office alone came more than three hundred pounds of paper that, on consideration, was condemned to pulp as not worth keeping.

The pamphlet I found must have been lying at the bottom of a bottom drawer—it was on top of the salvage basket. If the lady, or gentleman, who sent it to the *People* will communicate with me I will gladly pay her (or him) two hundred and fifty English pounds.

As literature it is nothing but a piece of pretentious nonsense written by one of those idle dabblers in "natural philosophy" who rushed into print on the slightest provocation in the eighteenth century. But the significance of it is formidable.

It makes me afraid.

The author of my pamphlet had attempted to tickle his way into public notice with the feather of his pen by writing an account of a monster captured by a boatman fishing several miles out of Brighthelmstone in the county of Sussex in the summer of the year 1745.

The name of the author was the Reverend Arthur Titty. I see him as one of those pushing, self-assertive vicars of the period, a rider to hounds, a purple-faced consumer of prodigious quantities of old port; a man of independent fortune, trying to persuade the world and himself that he was a deep thinker and a penetrating observer of the mysterious works of God.

I should never have taken the trouble to pocket his *Account of a Strange Monster Captured Near Brighthelmstone in the County of*

Sussex on August 6th in the Year of Our Lord 1745 if it had not been coincidence of the date: I was born on August 6. So I pushed the yellowed, damp-freckled pages into the breast pocket of my battle-dress, and thought no more about them until April 1947, when a casual remark sent me running, yelling like a maniac, to the cupboard in which my old uniforms were hanging.

The pamphlet was still in its pocket.

I shall not waste your time or strain your patience with the Reverend Arthur Titty's turgid, high-falutin' prose or his references to *De rerum*—this, that and the other. I propose to give you the unadorned facts in the very queer case of the Brighthelmstone monster.

Brighthelmstone is now known as Brighton—a large, popular, prosperous holiday resort delightfully situated on the coast of Sussex by the Downs. But in the Reverend Titty's day it was an obscure fishing village.

If a fisherman named Hodge had not had an unlucky night on August 5, 1745, on the glass-smooth sea off Brighthelmstone, this story would never have been told. He had gone out with his brother-in-law, George Rodgers, and they had caught nothing but a few small and valueless fishes. Hodge was desperate. He was notorious in the village as a spendthrift and a drunkard, and it was suspected that he had a certain connection with a barmaid at the Smack Inn—it was alleged that she had a child by him in the spring of the following year. He had scored up fifteen shillings for beer and needed a new net. It is probable, therefore, that Hodge stayed out in his boat until after the dawn of August 6 because he feared to face his wife—who also, incidentally, was with child.

At last, glum, sullen, and thoroughly out of sorts, he prepared to go home.

And then, he said, there was something like a splash—only it was not a splash: it was rather like the bursting of a colossal bubble: and there, in the sea, less than ten yards from his boat, was the monster, floating.

George Rodgers said: "By gogs, Jack Hodge, yon's a man!"

"Man? How can 'a be a man? Where could a man come from?"

The creature that had appeared with the sound of a bursting bubble drifted closer, and Hodge, reaching out with a boat hook, caught it under the chin and pulled it to the side of the boat.

"That be a merman," he said, "and no Christian man. Look at 'un, all covered wi' snakes and fire-drakes, and yellow like a slug's belly. By the Lord, George Rodgers, this might be the best night's fishing I ever did if it's alive, please the Lord! For if it is I can sell that for better money than ever I got for my best catch this last twenty years, or any other fisherman either. Lend a hand, Georgie-boy, and let's have a feel of it."

George Rodgers said: "That's alive, by hell—look now, and see the way the blood runs down where the gaff went home."

"Haul it in, then, and don't stand there gaping like a puddock."

They dragged the monster into the boat. It was shaped like a man and covered from throat to ankle with brilliantly colored images of strange monsters. A green, red, yellow and blue thing like a lizard sprawled between breast bone and navel. Great serpents were coiled above its legs. A smaller snake, red and blue, was picked out on the monster's right arm: the snake's tail covered the forefinger and its head was hidden in the armpit. On the left-hand side of its chest there was a big heart-shaped design in flaming scarlet. A great bird like an eagle in red and green spread its wings from shoulder-blade to shoulder-blade, and a red fox chased six blue rabbits from the middle of his spine into some unknown hiding place between his legs. There were lobsters, fishes, and insects on his left arm and on his right buttock a devilfish sprawled, encircling the lower part of his body with its tentacles. The back of his right hand was decorated with a butterfly in yellow, red, indigo and green. Low down, in the center of the throat, where the bone begins, there was a strange, incomprehensible, evil-looking symbol.

The monster was naked. In spite of its fantastic appearance it was so unmistakably a male human being that George Rodgers—a weak-minded but respectable man—covered it with a sack. Hodge prised open the monster's mouth to look at its teeth, having warned his brother-in-law to stand by with an axe in case of emergency. The man-shaped creature out of the sea had red gums, a red tongue, and teeth as white as sugar.

They forced it to swallow a little gin—Hodge always had a flask of gin in the boat—and it came to life with a great shudder, and cried out in a strange voice, opening wild black eyes and looking crazily left and right.

"Tie that up. You tie that's hands while I tie that's feet," said Hodge.

The monster offered no resistance.

"Throw 'un back," said George Rodgers, suddenly overtaken by a nameless dread. "Throw 'un back, Jack, I say!"

But Hodge said: "You be mazed, George Rodgers, you born fool. I can sell 'e for twenty-five golden guineas. Throw 'un back? I'll throw 'ee back for a brass farthing, tha' witless fool!"

There was no wind. The two fishermen pulled for the shore. The monster lay in the bilge, rolling its eyes. The silly, good-natured Rodgers offered it a crust of bread which it snapped up so avidly that it bit his finger to the bone. Then Hodge tried to cram a wriggling live fish into its mouth, but "the monster spat it out *pop*, like a cork out of a bottle, saving your Honor's presence."

Brighthelmstone boiled over with excitement when they landed. Even the Reverend Arthur Titty left his book and his breakfast, clapped on his three-cornered hat, picked up his cane, and went down to the fish-market to see what was happening. They told him that Hodge had caught a monster, a fish that looked like a man, a merman, a hypogriff, a sphinx—heaven knows what. The crowd parted and Titty came face to face with the monster.

Although the monster understood neither Hebrew, Greek, Latin, Italian nor French, it was obvious that it was a human being, or something remarkably like one. This was evident in its manner of wrinkling its forehead, narrowing its eyes, and demonstrating that it was capable of understanding—or of wanting to understand, which is the same thing. But it could not speak; it could only cry out incoherently and it was obviously greatly distressed. The Reverend Arthur Titty said: "Oafs, ignorant louts! This is no

THE BRIGHTON MONSTER 25

sea monster, you fools, no *lusus naturae*, but an unfortunate ship-wrecked mariner."

According to the pamphlet, Hodge said: "Your Reverence, begging your Reverence's pardon, how can that be, since for the past fortnight there has been no breath of wind and no foreign vessel in these parts? If this be an unfortunate shipwrecked mariner, where is the wreck of his ship, and where was it wrecked? I humbly ask your Reverence how he appeared as you might say out of a bubble without warning on the face of the water, floating. And if your Honor will take the trouble to observe this unhappy creature's skin your Reverence will see that it shows no signs of having been immersed for any considerable period in the ocean."

I do not imagine for a moment that this is what Hodge really said: he probably muttered the substance of the argument in the form of an angry protest emphasized by a bitten-off oath or two. However, the Reverend Arthur Titty perceived that what the fisherman said was "not without some show of reason" and said that he proposed to take the monster to his house for examination.

Hodge protested vigorously. It was his monster, he said, because he had caught it in the open sea with his own hands, in his own boat, and parson or no parson, if Titty were the Archbishop himself, an Englishman had his rights. After some altercation, in the course of which the monster fainted, the Reverend Arthur Titty gave Hodge a silver crown piece for the loan of the monster for philosophical observation. They poured a few buckets of sea water over the monster which came back to consciousness with a tremulous sigh. This was regarded as positive proof of its watery origin. Then it was carried to Titty's house on a hurdle.

It rejected salt water as a drink, preferring fresh water or wine, and ate cooked food, expressing, with unmistakable grimaces, a distaste for raw fish and meat. It was put to bed on a heap of clean straw and covered with a blanket which was kept moistened with sea water. Soon the monster of Brighthelmstone revived and appeared desirous of walking. It could even make sounds reminiscent of human speech.

The Reverend Arthur Titty covered its nakedness under a pair of his old breeches and one of his old shirts . . . as if it had not been grotesque-looking enough before.

He weighed it, measured it, and bled it to discover whether it was thick or thin-blooded, cold or hot-blooded. According to Titty's fussy little account the monster was about five feet one and three-quarter inches tall. It weighed exactly one hundred and nineteen pounds, and walked upright. It possessed unbelievable strength and superhuman agility. On one occasion the Reverend Arthur Titty took it out for a walk on the end of a leather leash. The local blacksmith, one of Hodge's boon companions, who was notorious for his gigantic muscular power and bad temper— he was later to achieve nationwide fame as Clifford, who broke the arm of the champion wrestler of Yorkshire—accosted the Reverend Arthur Titty outside his smithy and said: "Ah, so that's Hodge's catch as you stole from him. Let me feel of it to see if it be real," and he pinched the monster's shoulder very cruelly with one of his great hands—hands that could snap horseshoes and twist iron bars into spirals. The inevitable crowd of children and gaping villagers witnessed the event. The monster picked up the two-hundred-pound blacksmith and threw him into a heap of scrap iron three yards away. For an anxious second or two Titty thought that the monster was going to run amok, for its entire countenance changed; the nostrils quivered, the eyes shone with fierce intelligence, and from its open mouth there came a weird cry. Then the creature relapsed into heavy dejection and let itself be led home quietly, while the astonished blacksmith, bruised and bleeding, limped back to his anvil with the shocked air of a man who has seen the impossible come to pass.

Yet, the monster was an extremely sick monster. It ate little, sometimes listlessly chewing the same mouthful for fifteen minutes. It liked to squat on its haunches and stare unblinkingly at the sea. It was assumed that it was homesick for its native element, and so it was soused at intervals with buckets of brine and given a large tub of sea water to sleep in if it so desired. A learned doctor of medicine came all the way from Dover to examine it and pronounced it human; unquestionably an air-breathing mammal. But

so were whales and crocodiles breathers of air that lived in the
water.

Hodge, alternately threatening and whimpering, claimed his
property. The Reverend Arthur Titty called in his lawyer, who so
bewildered the unfortunate fisherman with Latin quotations, legal
jargon, dark hints and long words that, cursing and growling, he
scrawled a cross in lieu of a signature at the foot of a document
in which he agreed to relinquish all claim on the monster in consideration of the sum of seven guineas, payable on the spot. Seven
guineas was a great deal of money for a fisherman in those days.
Hodge had never seen so many gold pieces in a heap, and had
never owned one. Then a traveling showman visited the Reverend
Arthur Titty and offered him twenty-five guineas for the monster, which Titty refused. The showman spoke of the matter in
the Smack, and Hodge, who had been drunk for a week, behaved
"like one demented," as Titty wrote in a contemptuous footnote.
He made a thorough nuisance of himself, demanding the balance
of the twenty-five guineas which were his by rights, was arrested
and fined for riotous conduct. Then he was put in the stocks as
an incorrigible drunkard, and the wicked little urchins of Brighthelmstone threw fish-guts at him.

Let out of the stocks with a severe reprimand, smelling horribly
of dead fish, Hodge went to the Smack and ordered a quart of
strong ale, which came in a heavy can. Rodgers, to whom Hodge
had given only twelve shillings, came in for his modest morning
draft, and told Hodge that he was nothing better than a damned
rogue. He claimed half of the seven golden guineas. Hodge, having
drunk his quart, struck Rodgers with the can, and broke his skull;
for which he was hanged not long afterwards.

The Brighthelmstone monster was an unlucky monster.

The Reverend Arthur Titty also suffered. After the killing of
Rodgers and the hanging of Hodge the fishermen began to hate
him. Heavy stones were thrown against his shutters at night.
Someone set fire to one of his haystacks. This must have given
Titty something to think about, for rick-burning was a hanging
matter, and one may as well hang for a parson as for a haystack. He

made up his mind to go to London and live in politer society. So he was uprooted by the monster. The fishermen hated the monster too. They regarded it as a sort of devil. But the monster did not care. It was languishing, dying of a mysterious sickness. Curious sores had appeared at various points on the monster's body—they began as little white bumps such as one gets from stinging-nettles, and slowly opened and would not close. The looseness of the skin, now, lent the dragons and fishes a disgustingly lifelike look: as the monster breathed, they writhed. A veterinary surgeon poured melted pitch on the sores. The Reverend Titty kept it well soaked in sea water and locked it in a room, because it had shown signs of wanting to escape.

At last, nearly three months after its first appearance in Bright-helmstone, the monster escaped. An old manservant, Alan English, unlocked the door, in the presence of the Reverend Arthur Titty, to give the monster its daily mess of vegetables and boiled meat. As the key turned, the door was flung open with such violence that English fell forward into the room—his hand was still on the doorknob—and the monster ran out, crying aloud in a high, screaming voice. The Reverend Arthur Titty caught it by the shoulder, whereupon he was whisked away like a leaf in the wind and lay stunned at the end of the passage. The monster ran out of the house. Three responsible witnesses—Rebecca North, Herbert George and Abraham Herris (or Harris)—saw it running towards the sea, stark naked, although a northeast wind was blowing. The two men ran after it, and Rebecca North followed as fast as she could. The monster ran straight into the bitter water and began to swim, its arms and legs vibrating like the wings of an insect. Herbert George saw it plunge into the green heart of a great wave, and then the heavy rain fell like a curtain and the Brighthelmstone monster was never seen again.

It had never spoken. In the later stages of its disease its teeth had fallen out. With one of these teeth—probably a canine—it had scratched marks on the dark oak panels of the door of the room in which it was confined. These marks the Reverend Arthur Titty faithfully copied and reproduced in his pamphlet.

The Brighthelmstone fishermen said that the sea devil had gone back where it belonged, down to the bottom of the sea to its palace built of the bones of lost Christian sailors. Sure enough, half an hour after the monster disappeared there was a terrible storm, and many seamen lost their lives. In a month or so Titty left Brighthelmstone for London. The city swallowed him. He published his pamphlet in 1746—a bad year for natural philosophy, because the ears of England were still full of the Jacobite rebellion of '45.

Poor Titty! If he could have foreseen the real significance of the appearance of the monster of Brighthelmstone he would have died happy . . . in a lunatic asylum.

Nobody would have believed him.

Now in April 1947 I had the good fortune to meet one of my oldest and dearest friends, a colonel in Intelligence who, for obvious reasons, must remain anonymous, although he is supposed to be in retirement now and wears civilian clothes, elegantly cut in the narrow-sleeved style of the late nineteen-twenties, and rather the worse for wear. The colonel is in many ways a romantic character, something like Rudyard Kipling's Strickland Sahib. He has played many strange parts in his time, that formidable old warrior; and his quick black eyes, disturbingly Asiatic-looking under the slackly-drooping eyelids, have seen more than you and I will ever see.

He never talks about his work. An Intelligence officer who talks ceases automatically to be an Intelligence officer. A good deal of his conversation is of sport, manly sport—polo, pig-sticking, cricket, rugby football, hunting, and, above all, boxing and wrestling. I imagine that the colonel, who has lived underground in disguise for so many years of his life, finds relief in the big wide-open games in which a man must meet his opponent face to face yet may, without breaking the rules, play quick tricks.

We were drinking coffee and smoking cigarettes after dinner in my flat and he was talking about oriental wrestling. He touched on wrestling technique among the Afghans and in the Deccan, and spoke with admiration of Gama, the Western Indian wrestler, still a rock-crusher at an age when most men are shivering in slippers by the fire, who beat Zbyszko; remarked on a southeastern Indian named Patil who could knock a strong man senseless with the knuckle of his left thumb; and went on to Chinese wrestlers, especially Mongolians, who are tremendously heavy and powerful, and use their feet. A good French-Canadian lumberjack (the colonel said), accustomed to dancing on rolling logs in a rushing river, could do dreadful things with his legs and feet, like the Tiger of Quebec, who in a scissors-hold killed Big Ted Glass of Detroit. In certain kinds of wrestling size and weight were essential, said the colonel. The Japanese wrestlers of the heavy sort—the ones that weighed three or four hundred pounds and looked like pigs— those big ones that started on all fours and went through a series of ritual movements; they had to be enormously heavy. In fact the heavier they were the better.

"No, Gerald my lad, give me ju-jitsu," he said. "There is no one on earth who can defeat a master of ju-jitsu—except someone who takes him by surprise. Of course, a scientific boxer, getting a well-placed punch in first, would put him out for the count. But the real adept develops such wonderful coordination of hand and eye that if he happens to be expecting it he can turn to his own advantage even the lightning punch of a wizard like Jimmy Wilde. He could give away eight stone to Joe Louis and make him look silly. Georges Hackenschmidt, for instance, is one of the greatest catch-as-catch-can wrestlers that ever lived, and one of the strongest men of his day. But I question whether he, wrestling catch, might have stood up against Yukio Tani? Oh, by the way, speaking of Yukio Tani, did you ever hear of a wrestler called Sato?"

"I can't say that I have. Why? Should I have heard of him?"

"Why, he is, or was, a phenomenon. I think he was a better wrestler than Tani. My idea was to take him all round the world and challenge all comers—boxers, wrestlers, even fencers, to stand up against him for ten minutes. He was unbelievable. Furthermore, he *looked* so frightful. I won a hundred and fifty quid on him at Singapore in 1938. He took on four of the biggest and best boxers and wrestlers we could lay our hands on and floored the whole lot in seven minutes by the clock. Just a minute, I've got a picture in my wallet. I keep it because it looks so damn funny. Look."

The colonel handed me a dog-eared photograph of an oddly assorted group. There was a hairy mammoth of a man, obviously a wrestler, standing with his arms folded so that his biceps looked like coconuts, beside another man, almost as big, but with the scrambled features of a rough-and-tumble bruiser. There was one blond grinning man who looked like a light heavyweight, and a beetle-browed middleweight with a bulldog jaw. The colonel was standing in the background, smiling in a fatherly way. In the foreground, smiling into the camera, stood a tiny Japanese. The top of his head was on a level with the big wrestler's breastbone, but he was more than half as broad as he was tall. He was all chest and arms. The knuckles of his closed hands touched his knees. I took the picture to the light and looked more closely. The photographer's flashbulb had illuminated every detail. Sato had made himself even more hideous with tattooing. He was covered with things that creep and crawl, real and fabulous. A dragon snarled on his stomach. Snakes were coiled about his legs. Another snake wound itself about his right arm from forefinger to armpit. The other arm was covered with angry-looking lobsters and goggle-eyed fishes, and on the left breast there was the conventionalized shape of a heart.

It was then that I uttered an astonished oath and went running to look for my old uniform, which I found, with the Reverend Arthur Titty's pamphlet still in the inside breast pocket. The colonel asked me what the devil was the matter with me. I smoothed out the pamphlet and gave it to him without a word.

He looked at it, and said: "How very extraordinary!" Then he put away his eyeglass and put on a pair of spectacles; peered intently at the smudged and ragged drawing of the Brighthelmstone monster, compared it with the photograph of Sato, and said to me: "I have come across some pretty queer things in my time, but I'm damned if I know what to make of this."

"Tell me," I said, "was your Sato tattooed behind? And if so, in what way?"

Without hesitation the colonel said: "A red-and-green hawk stooping between the shoulder-blades, a red fox chasing six blue-gray rabbits down his spine, and an octopus on the right buttock throwing out tentacles that went round to the belly. Why?"

Then I opened Titty's pamphlet and put my finger on the relevant passage. The colonel read it and changed color. But he said nothing. I said: "This is the damnedest coincidence. There's another thing. This so-called monster of Brighton scratched something on the door of the room where he was locked up, and the old parson took a pencil rubbing of it. Turn over four or five pages and you'll see a copy of it."

The colonel found the page. The spongy old paper was worn into holes, blurred by time and the dampness of lumber-rooms and the moisture of my body. He said: "It looks like Japanese. But no Japanese would write like that surely . . ."

"Remember," I said, "that the Brighton monster scratched its message with one of its own teeth on the panel of an oak door. Allow for that; allow for the fact that it was weak and sick; take into consideration the grain of the wood; and then see what you make of it."

The colonel looked at the inscription for ten long minutes, copying it several times from several different angles. At last he said: "This says: *I was asleep. I thought that it was all a bad dream from which I should awake and find myself by the side of my wife. Now I know that it is not a dream. I am sick in the head. Pity me, poor Sato, who went to sleep in one place and awoke in another. I cannot live any more. I must die. Hiroshima 1945.*"

"What do you make of that?" I asked.

The Colonel said: "I don't know. I only know the bare facts about Sato because, as I have already told you, I was trying to find him. (a) He had a wife, and a home somewhere in Hiroshima. (b) He was in the Japanese Navy, and he went on leave in August 1945. (c) Sato disappeared off the face of the earth when they dropped that damned atom bomb. (d) This is unquestionably a picture of Sato—the greatest little wrestler the world has ever known. (e) The description of the tattooing on the back of this monster tal-

lies exactly with Sato's . . . I don't know quite what to make of it.
Sato, you know, was a Christian. He counted the years the Christian way. *Hiroshima 1945*. I wonder!"

"What do you wonder?"

"Why," said the colonel, "there can't be the faintest shadow of
a doubt that Sato got the middle part of the blast of that frightful atom bomb when we dropped it on Hiroshima. You may or
may not have heard of Dr. Sant's crazy theories concerning time
in relation to speed. Now imagine that you happen to be caught up
—without disintegrating—in a species of air-pocket on the fringe
of an atomic blast and are flung away a thousand times faster than
if you had been fired out of a cannon. Imagine it. According to the
direction in which you happen to be thrown you may find yourself
in the middle of tomorrow or on the other side of yesterday. Don't
laugh at me. I may have been frying my brains in the tropics most
of my life, and I may be crazy; but I've learned to believe all kinds
of strange things. My opinion is that my poor little Sato was liter-
ally blown back two hundred years in time."

I said: "But why blown backwards only in time? How do you
account for his being struck by the blast in Hiroshima and ending
in Brighton?"

"I'm no mathematician," said the colonel, "but as I understand,
the earth is perpetually spinning and space is therefore shifting all
the time. If you, for example, could stand absolutely still, here,
now, where you are, while the earth moved—if you stood still only
for one hour, you'd find yourself in Budapest. Do you understand
what I mean? That atomic blast picked little Sato up and threw him
back in time. When you come to think of that, and remember all
the curious monsters they used to exhibit in Bartholomew's Fair
during the eighteenth century—when you think of all the mer-
maids, monsters, and mermen that they picked out of the sea and
showed on fairgrounds until they died . . . it makes you think."

"It makes you think."

"Do you observe, by the way," said the colonel, pointing to the
Reverend Titty's pamphlet, "that poor little Sato was sick with
running sores, and that his teeth were falling out? Radioactivity

poisoning: these are the symptoms. Poor Sato! Can you wonder why he got desperate and simply chucked himself back into the sea to sink or swim? Put yourself in his position. You go to sleep in Hiroshima, in August 1945 and then—*Whoof!*—you find yourself in Brighton, in November 1745. No wonder the poor wretch couldn't speak. That shock would be enough to paralyze anyone's tongue. It scares me, Kersh, my boy—it puts a match to trains of thought of the most disturbing nature. It makes me remember that past and future are all one. I shall really worry, in future, when I have a nightmare . . . one of those nightmares in which you find yourself lost, struck dumb, completely bewildered in a place you've never seen before—a place out of this world. God have mercy on us, I wish they'd never thought of that disgusting secret weapon!"

You are free to argue the point, to speculate and to draw your own conclusions. But this is the end (or, God forbid, the beginning) of the story of the Brighton monster.

MEN WITHOUT BONES

W̲ᴇ were loading bananas into the *Claire Dodge* at Puerto
Pobre, when a feverish little fellow came aboard. Everyone stepped aside to let him pass—even the soldiers who guard the
port with nickel-plated Remington rifles, and who go barefoot but
wear polished leather leggings. They stood back from him because
they believed that he was afflicted-of-God, mad; harmless but dangerous; best left alone.

All the time the naphtha flares were hissing, and from the hold
came the reverberation of the roaring voice of the foreman of the
gang down below crying: "Fruta! Fruta! *FRUTA!*" The leader of the
dock gang bellowed the same cry, throwing down stem after stem
of brilliant green bananas. The occasion would be memorable for
this, if for nothing else—the magnificence of the night, the bronze
of the Negro foreman shining under the flares, the jade green of
that fruit, and the mixed odors of the waterfront. Out of one stem
of bananas ran a hairy gray spider, which frightened the crew and
broke the banana-chain, until a Nicaraguan boy, with a laugh,
killed it with his foot. It was harmless, he said.

It was about then that the madman came aboard, unhindered,
and asked me: "Bound for where?"

He spoke quietly and in a carefully modulated voice; but there
was a certain blank, lost look in his eyes that suggested to me that I
keep within ducking distance of his restless hands which, now that I
think of them, put me in mind of that gray, hairy, bird-eating spider.

"Mobile, Alabama," I said.

"Take me along?" he asked.

"None of my affair. Sorry. Passenger myself," I said. "The skip-
per's ashore. Better wait for him on the wharf. He's the boss."

"Would you happen, by any chance, to have a drink about you?"

Giving him some rum, I asked: "How come they let you
aboard?"

"I'm not crazy," he said. "Not actually . . . a little fever, nothing more. Malaria, dengue fever, jungle fever, rat-bite fever. Feverish country, this, and others of the same nature. Allow me to introduce myself. My name is Goodbody, Doctor of Science of Osbaldeston University. Does it convey nothing to you? No? Well then; I was assistant to Professor Yeoward. Does *that* convey anything to you?"

I said: "Yeoward, Professor Yeoward? Oh yes. He was lost, wasn't he, somewhere in the upland jungle beyond the source of the Amer River?"

"Correct!" cried the little man who called himself Goodbody. "I saw him get lost."

Fruta!—Fruta!—Fruta!—Fruta! came the voices of the men in the hold. There was rivalry between their leader and the big black stevedore ashore. The flares spluttered. The green bananas came down. And a kind of sickly sigh came out of the jungle, off the rotting river—not a wind, not a breeze—something like the foul breath of high fever.

Trembling with eagerness and, at the same time, shaking with fever chills, so that he had to use two hands to raise his glass to his lips—even so, he spilled most of the rum—Doctor Goodbody said: "For God's sake, get me out of this country—take me to Mobile—hide me in your cabin!"

"I have no authority," I said, "but you are an American citizen; you can identify yourself; the consul will send you home."

"No doubt. But that would take time. The consul thinks I am crazy too. And if I don't get away, I fear that I really will go out of my mind. Can't you help me? I'm afraid."

"Come on, now," I said. "No one shall hurt you while I'm around. What are you afraid of?"

"Men without bones," he said, and there was something in his voice that stirred the hairs on the back of my neck. "Little fat men without bones!"

I wrapped him in a blanket, gave him some quinine, and let him sweat and shiver for a while, before I asked, humoring him: "What men without bones?"

He talked in fits and starts in his fever, his reason staggering just this side of delirium:

". . . What men without bones? . . . They are nothing to be afraid of, actually. It is they who are afraid of you. You can kill them with your boot, or with a stick. . . . They are something like jelly. No, it is not really fear—it is the nausea, the disgust they inspire. It overwhelms. It paralyzes! I have seen a jaguar, I tell you—a full-grown jaguar—stand frozen, while they clung to him, in hundreds, and ate him up alive! Believe me, I saw it. Perhaps it is some oil they secrete, some odor they give out . . . I don't know . . ."

Then, weeping, Doctor Goodbody said: "Oh, nightmare—nightmare—nightmare! To think of the depths to which a noble creature can be degraded by hunger! Horrible, horrible!"

"Some debased form of life that you found in the jungle above the source of the Amer?" I suggested. "Some degenerate kind of anthropoid?"

"No, no, no. *Men!* Now surely you remember Professor Yeoward's technological expedition?"

"It was lost," I said.

"All but me," he said. ". . . We had bad luck. At the Anaña rapids we lost two canoes, half our supplies and most of our instruments. And also Doctor Terry, and Jack Lambert, and eight of our carriers. . . .

"Then we were in Ahu territory where the Indians use poison darts, but we made friends with them and bribed them to carry our stuff westward through the jungle . . . because, you see, all science starts with a guess, a rumor, an old wives' tale; and the object of Professor Yeoward's expedition was to investigate a series of Indian folk tales that tallied. Legends of a race of gods that came down from the sky in a great flame when the world was very young. . . .

"Line by crisscross line, and circle by concentric circle, Yeoward localized the place in which these tales had their root—an unexplored place that has no name because the Indians refuse to give it a name, it being what they call a 'bad place'."

His chills subsiding and his fever abating, Doctor Goodbody

spoke calmly and rationally now. He said, with a short laugh: "I don't know why, whenever I get a touch of fever, the memory of those boneless men comes back in a nightmare to give me the horrors. . . .

"So, we went to look for the place where the gods came down in flame out of the night. The little tattooed Indians took us to the edge of the Ahu territory and then put down their packs and asked for their pay, and no consideration would induce them to go further. We were going, they said, to a very bad place. Their chief, who had been a great man in his day, sign-writing with a twig, told us that he had strayed there once, and drew a picture of something with an oval body and four limbs, at which he spat before rubbing it out with his foot in the dirt. Spiders? we asked. Crabs? What?

"So we were forced to leave what we could not carry with the old chief against our return, and go on unaccompanied, Yeoward and I, through thirty miles of the rottenest jungle in the world. We made about a quarter of a mile in a day . . . a pestilential place! When that stinking wind blows out of the jungle, I smell nothing but death, and panic. . . .

"But, at last, we cut our way to the plateau and climbed the slope, and there we saw something marvelous. It was something that had been a gigantic machine. Originally it must have been a pear-shaped thing, at least a thousand feet long and, in its widest part, six hundred feet in diameter. I don't know of what metal it had been made, because there was only a dusty outline of a hull and certain ghostly remains of unbelievably intricate mechanisms to prove that it had ever been. We could not guess from where it had come; but the impact of its landing had made a great valley in the middle of the plateau.

"It was the discovery of the age! It proved that, countless ages ago, this planet had been visited by people from the stars! Wild with excitement, Yeoward and I plunged into this fabulous ruin. But whatever we touched fell away to fine powder.

"At last, on the third day, Yeoward found a semicircular plate of some extraordinarily hard metal, which was covered with the most maddeningly familiar diagrams. We cleaned it, and for twenty-four hours, scarcely pausing to eat and drink, Yeoward studied it. And, then, before the dawn of the fifth day he awoke me, with a great cry, and said: 'It's a map, a map of the heavens, and a chart of a course from Mars to Earth!'

"And he showed me how those ancient explorers of space had proceeded from Mars to Earth, via the moon. . . . To crash on this naked plateau in this green hell of a jungle? I wondered. 'Ah, but was it a jungle then?' said Yeoward. 'This may have happened five million years ago!'

"I said: 'Oh, but surely! it took only a few hundred years to bury Rome. How could this thing have stayed above ground for five thousand years, let alone five million?' Yeoward said: 'It didn't. The earth swallows things and regurgitates them. This is a volcanic region. One little upheaval can swallow a city, and one tiny peristalsis in the bowels of the earth can bring its remains to light again a million years later. So it must have been with the machine from Mars . . .'

"'I wonder who was inside it,' I said. Yeoward replied: 'Very likely some utterly alien creatures that couldn't tolerate the Earth, and died, or else were killed in the crash. No skeleton could survive such a space of time.'

"So, we built up the fire, and Yeoward went to sleep. Having slept, I watched. Watched for what? I didn't know. Jaguars, peccaries, snakes? None of these beasts climbed up to the plateau; there was nothing for them up there. Still, unaccountably, I was afraid.

"There was the weight of ages on the place. *Respect old age*, one is told. . . . The greater the age, the deeper the respect, you might say. But it is not respect; it is dread, it is fear of time and death, sir! . . . I must have dozed, because the fire was burning low—I had been most careful to keep it alive and bright—when I caught my first glimpse of the boneless men.

"Starting up, I saw, at the rim of the plateau, a pair of eyes that picked up luminosity from the fading light of the fire. *A jaguar*, I thought, and took up my rifle. But it could not have been a jaguar because, when I looked left and right I saw that the plateau was ringed with pairs of shining eyes . . . as it might be, a collar of opals; and there came to my nostrils an odor of God knows what.

"Fear has its smell as any animal-trainer will tell you. Sickness has its smell—ask any nurse. These smells compel healthy animals to fight or to run away. This was a combination of the two, plus a stink of vegetation gone bad. I fired at the pair of eyes I had first seen. Then, all the eyes disappeared while, from the jungle, there came a chattering and a twittering of monkeys and birds, as the echoes of the shot went flapping away.

"And then, thank God, the dawn came. I should not have liked to see by artificial light the thing I had shot between the eyes.

"It was gray and, in texture, tough and gelatinous. Yet, in form, externally, it was not unlike a human being. It had eyes, and there were either vestiges—or rudiments—of head, and neck, and a kind of limbs.

"Yeoward told me that I must pull myself together; overcome my 'childish revulsion,' as he called it; and look into the nature of the beast. I may say that he kept a long way away from it when I opened it. It was my job as zoologist of the expedition, and I had to do it. Microscopes and other delicate instruments had been lost with the canoes. I worked with a knife and forceps. And found? Nothing: a kind of digestive system enclosed in very tough jelly, a rudimentary nervous system, and a brain about the size of a walnut. The entire creature, stretched out, measured four feet.

"In a laboratory I could tell you, perhaps, something about it . . . with an assistant or two, to keep me company. As it was, I did what I could with a hunting-knife and forceps, without dyes or microscope, swallowing my nausea—it was a nauseating thing!— memorizing what I found. But, as the sun rose higher, the thing liquefied, melted, until by nine o'clock there was nothing but a glutinous gray puddle, with two green eyes swimming in it. . . . And those eyes—I can see them now—burst with a thick *pop*, making a detestable sticky ripple in that puddle of corruption. . . .

"After that, I went away for a while. When I came back, the sun had burned it all away, and there was nothing but something like what you see after a dead jellyfish has evaporated on a hot beach. Slime. Yeoward had a white face when he asked me: 'What the

devil is it?' I told him that I didn't know, that it was something outside my experience, and that although I pretended to be a man of
science with a detached mind, nothing would induce me ever to
touch one of the things again.

"Yeoward said: 'You're getting hysterical, Goodbody. Adopt the
proper attitude. God knows, we are not here for the good of our
health. Science, man, science! Not a day passes but some doctor
pokes his fingers into fouler things than that!' I said: 'Don't you
believe it. Professor Yeoward, I have handled and dissected some
pretty queer things in my time, but this is something repulsive. I
have nerves? I dare say. Maybe we should have brought a psychia-
trist . . . I notice, by the way, that you aren't too anxious to come
close to me after I've tampered with that thing. I'll shoot one with
pleasure, but if you want to investigate it, try it yourself and see!'

"Yeoward said that he was deeply occupied with his metal plate.
There was no doubt, he told me, that this machine that had been
had come from Mars. But, evidently, he preferred to keep the fire
between himself and me, after I had touched that abomination of
hard jelly.

"Yeoward kept himself to himself, rummaging in the ruin. I
went about my business, which was to investigate forms of animal
life. I do not know what I might I have found, if I had had—I don't
say the courage, because I didn't lack that—if I had had some company. Alone, my nerve broke.

"It happened one morning. I went into the jungle that surrounded us, trying to swallow the fear that choked me, and drive
away the sense of revulsion that not only made me want to turn
and run, but made me afraid to turn my back even to get away.
You may or may not know that, of all the beasts that live in that
jungle, the most impregnable is the sloth. He finds a stout limb,
climbs out on it, and hangs from it by his twelve steely claws; a
tardigrade that lives on leaves. Your tardigrade is so tenacious that
even in death, shot through the heart, it will hang on to its branch.
It has an immensely tough hide covered by an impenetrable coat
of coarse, matted hair. A panther or a jaguar is helpless against the
passive resistance of such a creature. It finds itself a tree, which it

does not leave until it has eaten every leaf, and chooses for a sleeping place a branch exactly strong enough to bear its weight.

"In this detestable jungle, on one of my brief expeditions—brief, because I was alone and afraid—I stopped to watch a giant sloth hanging motionless from the largest bough of a half-denuded tree, asleep, impervious, indifferent. Then, out of that stinking green twilight came a horde of those jellyfish things. They *poured up* the tree, and writhed along the branch.

"Even the sloth, which generally knows no fear, was afraid. It tried to run away, hooked itself on to a thinner part of the branch, which broke. It fell, and at once was covered with a shuddering mass of jelly. Those boneless men do not bite: they suck. And, as they suck, their color changes from gray to pink and then to brown.

"But they are afraid of us. There is race-memory involved here. We repel them, and they repel us. When they became aware of my presence, they—I was going to say, ran away—they slid away, dissolved into the shadows that kept dancing and dancing and dancing under the trees. And the horror came upon me, so that I ran away, and arrived back at our camp, bloody about the face with thorns, and utterly exhausted.

"Yeoward was lancing a place in his ankle. A tourniquet was tied under his knee. Nearby lay a dead snake. He had broken its back with that same metal plate, but it had bitten him first. He said: 'What kind of a snake do you call this? I'm afraid it is venomous. I feel a numbness in my cheeks and around my heart, and I cannot feel my hands.'

"I said: 'Oh, my God! You've been bitten by a jararaca!'

"'And we have lost our medical supplies,' he said, with regret. 'And there is so much work left to do. Oh, dear me, dear me! . . . Whatever happens, my dear fellow, take *this* and get back.'

"And he gave me that semicircle of unknown metal as a sacred trust. Two hours later, he died. That night the circle of glowing eyes grew narrower. I emptied my rifle at it, time and again. At dawn, the boneless men disappeared.

"I heaped rocks on the body of Yeoward. I made a pylon, so that the men without bones could not get at him. Then—oh, so dreadfully lonely and afraid!—I shouldered my pack, and took my rifle and my machete, and ran away, down the trail we had covered. But I lost my way.

"Can by can of food, I shed weight. Then my rifle went, and my ammunition. After that, I threw away even my machete. A long time later, that semicircular plate became too heavy for me, so I tied it to a tree with liana vine, and went on.

"So I reached the Ahu territory, where the tattooed men nursed me and were kind to me. The women chewed my food for me, before they fed me, until I was strong again. Of the stores we have left there, I took only as much as I might need, leaving the rest as payment for guides and men to man the canoe down the river. And so I got back out of the jungle. . . .

"Please give me a little more rum." His hand was steady, now, as he drank, and his eyes were clear.

I said to him: "Assuming that what you say is true: these 'boneless men'—they were, I presume, the Martians? Yet it sounds unlikely, surely? Do invertebrates smelt hard metals and——"

"Who said anything about Martians?" cried Doctor Goodbody. "No, no, no! The Martians came here, adapted themselves to new conditions of life. Poor fellows, they changed, sank low; went through a whole new process—a painful process of evolution. What I'm trying to tell you, you fool, is that Yeoward and I did *not* discover Martians. Idiot, don't you see? *Those boneless things are men. We are Martians!*"

"BUSTO IS A GHOST,
TOO MEAN TO GIVE US A FRIGHT!"

T HERE was no such man as Shakmatko, but there really was Busto's lodging-house. It was just as I described it: a rickety, rotting, melancholy old house not far from New Oxford Street. The day came when Busto was kicked out: his lease had expired five years before, anyway. He fought like a trapped lynx to retain possession of the place, but the borough surveyor and the sanitary inspector had it in iron pincers. It was condemned and executed, torn to pieces, taken away in carts. And a good riddance, I say! Yet in retrospect one half regrets such demolitions. "Where is the house in which I lived?" one asks; and, walking past, looks up at the housebreakers, and sighs . . . "Ahhhhh. . . ."

Pah!

Time is more than a healer. It is a painter and decorator; a gilder and a glorifier. It converts the gritty particles of half-forgotten miseries into what sentimental old gentlemen call pearls of memory. Memory! Memory; fooey on memory! What a smooth liar it is, this memory! I have heard a shrapnel-tattered veteran recalling, with something suspiciously like sentimental regret, the mud of Passchendaele. I could feel twinges of pleasurable emotion about Busto's, if I let myself go. Yet I endured several miseries there. The place was chock-full of my pet aversions. Bedbugs, of which I have always had a nameless horror, came out at night and walked over me. For some reason unknown to science they never bit me. But other insects did. I used to lie in bed, too hungry and tired to sleep, and look out of the window over the black roofs, and listen to the faint, sad noises of the sleeping house; and marvel at the fearsome strength of vermin. Sandow, Hackenschmidt, gorillas, whales; they are nothing. For truly awful physical force watch insects. Compare the heart-bursting sprints of Olympic runners with the effortless speed of the spider; the bloody and ferocious gluttony of the wolf with that of the louse; the leap of the panther with the jump of the flea!

Busto's ghoulish presence filled the house. One worried about the rent. Sometimes I wrote verse at night, in true poetic style, by the light of a halfpenny candle—oh, most execrable verse, full of inspissated, treacly, heavy blue-black gloom. . . .

> In whose dim caves God and the ghosts of hope
> Hold panic orgy and forget the earth

—that kind of thing. What green caves? I forget. I think they were to be found in a "sea to sink in." What sea? Sink what? I don't remember. I also wrote a novel called *The Blonde and Oscar*. It was so sordid that it made publishers' readers scratch themselves. Compared with it, *L'Assommoir* was like something by Mrs. Humphry Ward, and *Jude the Obscure* a kind of *Winnie the Pooh*. Prostitutes? Millions of 'em. Degenerates? On every page. I left no stone unthrown; explored every drainpipe; took three deep breaths, attached a stone to my feet, exhaled, and sank to the bottom of the cesspit with a hideous gurgle. I tell you, publishers dropped it with muffled cries, and afterwards scrubbed their hands, like men who reach for pebbles on a beach and accidentally pick up something disgusting.

I was always having fights with other lodgers. My nerves were on edge. I was, in any case, a bit of an idiot, foolish with an uninspired foolishness—hell is full of such. I was unbelievably bumptious, arrogant, loudmouthed, moody, quarrelsome, bull-headed, touchy, gloomy, and proud in a silly kind of way. At the prospect of a roughhouse I boiled over with murderous joy. Only one man on earth inspired me with fear, and that was Busto.

Pio Busto used to cross himself before a lithograph of the Mona Lisa. He thought it represented the Virgin Mary. But in any case it was generally believed that Busto had no soul to save.

How small, how bent, and how virulent was Pio Busto, with his bulldog jaws, and his spine curved like a horseshoe! How diaboli-

cal were the little eyes, hard and black as basalt, that squinted out
of his pale, crunched-up face! Ragged, dirty, and lopsided, he had
the appearance of a handful of spoiled human material, crumpled
and thrown aside, accidentally dropped out of the cosmic dustbin.
It was said of him: "Busto is not human. Busto is not alive. Busto
is a ghost, too mean to give us a fright."

He really seemed to have no thought beyond wringing out
the rents of his abominable little furnished rooms. As soon as the
money was due, up popped Busto like the Devil in a legend. "My
landlorda gim*me* time to pay? Hah? Hooh!" If you asked him for
a match he would say: "Buy a box." There was a quality of doom
about his avarice. Professional bilkers took one look at Busto and
ran for their lives. Unemployed waiters—always habitual gamblers
and irrepressible mutterers-under-the-breath—remained silent in
his presence. He uttered few words, but his thin lips, corrugated
like the edges of scallop-shells, sawed off a whole repertoire of
formidable noises. His *Hooh!* expressed all the scorn in the world:
his *Hah?* was alive with malice.

About once a month he used to get drunk on red Lisbon—a
deadly and incalculable wine concocted of the squeezed-out scrap-
ings of rotted port-casks and laced with methylated spirits—a
terrible drink of doubtful origin, which smites the higher centers
as with a sandbag. It is otherwise known as lunatic's broth, or red
lizzie. Busto would consume bottles of it, and even offer small
saucers-full to his dog, Ouif. This, also, was a taciturn animal;
shaggy, half-deaf, suspicious and altogether badly formed. It was as
if some amateur Creator had tried to piece together a bull-terrier
with odds and ends of airedale, saluki, dachshund, and jackal. Ouif
shared his master's bed. Dogs have no esthetics, so it is easy for
them to be noble. Besides, it is physically necessary for a dog to
attach himself to somebody, if only a man like Busto, just as a man
must love some living thing, even a dog like Ouif.

Without Ouif, how could Busto have lived in the atmosphere
of hate with which he surrounded himself? He trailed a tradition
of pitilessness. Extortion was his *métier*. As he went his rounds, his
feet seemed to squeeze out of the squeaking stairs all the squeal-

ing notes in the gamut of human misery. Hopelessness had soaked into the pores of his ancient house; multitudes of passing tenants had left behind them the ghosts of their anguish and despair. Busto's was the step before the bottom. People came, lingered, clinging desperately as to a rock overhanging an abyss; then weakened and dropped out of sight. The time always came when Busto said: "Clear out before twellovaclock!" Almost every rent-day, some unhappy defaulter was thrown out.

My rent-day was Saturday. One Saturday evening I was hurrying in with the necessary nine-and-six, when I met Mr. Butts in the passage. He was an addresser of envelopes, a man with a booming voice, no shirt, and a monocle, most of whose earthly possessions were contained in a four-pound biscuit-tin. He was carrying this tin under his arm.

"Going?" I asked.

"Yes, my dear sir, I am," said Mr. Butts.

"Did Busto———"

"Of course. But he is sorry, now. You know, my dear sir, I never go out of my way to do anybody any harm, but people who wrong me always suffer for it afterwards. Busto throws me out into the street. Very good. An hour ago, his dog was run over. You see?"

"No! His dog?"

"Run over, my dear sir, by a taxi. Could you lend me fourpence?"

"Twopence?"

"A thousand thanks, my dear sir. . . . Good-bye, good-bye!"

The door slammed heavily. The rickety umbrella-stand vibrated to a standstill. Silence, darkness, and the evil odors of dampness and decay settled upon the passage. I went downstairs to the disused wash-house in which Busto lived and slept. I knocked. He tore the door open and cried. "Yes? Yes?" But when he saw me his face fell, and he said: "Oh, you. Hooh! I toughta you was da vet."

"The vet?" I said. "Why, is Ouif ill?"

"Yes."

"May I see him? I know a little bit about dogs."

"Yeh? Come in."

Ouif lay on Busto's bed, surrounded with pillows and covered with a blanket.

"Run over, eh?" I said.

"Ah-ah. How you know?"

Without replying, I lifted the blanket. Ouif was crushed, bent sideways. Practically unconscious, he breathed with a strenuous, groaning noise, his mouth wide open.

"Whacan I do?" asked Busto. "I touch 'im, it 'urts. You tella me. What I oughta do?"

I passed my hand gently down the dog's body. Ouif was smashed, finished. I replied: "I don't think there's anything much you can do."

"A hotawatta-bottle?"

"A hot-water bottle's no use. Wait till the vet comes."

"Hooh. But what I do? Dis is my dog. Brandy?"

"Don't be silly. Brandy'll make him cough, and it hurts him even to breathe."

"Hell!" exclaimed Busto, savagely.

I touched Ouif's stomach. He yelped sharply. I covered him again.

"How did it happen?"

Busto flung up his big, earth-colored fists in a helpless gesture. "Me, I go buya one-two bottla wine ova da road. Ouif run afta me. Dam taxi comes arounda da corner. Brr-rrr-oum! *Ffff!* Run aright ova da dog, withouta stop!" shouted Busto, opening and closing his hands with awful ferocity. "Hell, Ker-*ist!* If I getta holda diss fella. Gordamighty I tear 'im up a-to *bits!* Lissen; I tear outa diss fella's 'eart an' tear *dat* up a-to bits too! Yes!" shrieked Busto, striking at the wall with his knuckles and scattering flakes of distemper. "Lissen, you think 'e die, Ouif?"

"I'm afraid he might. All his stomach's crushed. And his ribs. All the bones——"

"*Basta, basta*, eh? Enough." Busto slouched over to the table, seized a bottle of wine and filled two tea-cups. "Drink!" he commanded, handing one to me; and emptied his cup at a gulp. I swallowed a mouthful of the wine. It seemed to vaporize in my stomach like water on a red-hot stove—*psssst!*—and the fumes rushed up to my head. Busto drank another cup, banging down the bottle.

"You like this dog, eh?" I said.

"I send my fraynd for the vet. Why don't dey come, dis vet?"

There was a knock at the front door. Busto rushed upstairs, and then came down followed by a wizened man who looked like a racing tipster, and a tall old man with a black bag.

"Dissa my dog."

"What happened?" asked the vet.

"Run over," said the little man, "I told yer, didn't I?"

"Well, let's have a look." The vet stooped, pulled back the blanket, and began to touch Ouif here and there with light, skillful hands; looked at his eyes, said "Hm!" and then shook his head.

"So?" said Busto.

"Nothing much to be done, I'm afraid. Quite hopeless."

"'E die, hah?"

"I'm afraid so. The best thing to do will be to put him out of his misery quickly."

"Misery?"

"I say, the kindest thing will be to put him to sleep."

"Kill 'im, 'e means," said the wizened man.

"Lissen," said Busto. "You mak this dog oright, I give you lotta money. Uh?"

"But I tell you, nothing can possibly be done. His pelvis is all smashed to——"

"Yes, yes, but lissen. You maka dis dog oright, I give you ten quid."

"Even if you offered me ten thousand pounds, Mister . . . er . . . I couldn't save your dog. I know how you feel, and I'm sorry. But I tell you, the kindest thing you can possibly do is put him quietly to sleep. He'll only go on suffering, to no purpose."

"Dammit, fifty quid!" cried Busto.

"I'm not considering money. If it were possible to help your dog, I would; but I can't."

"Dammit, a hundreda quid!" yelled Busto. "You tink I aina got no money? Hah! Look!" He dragged open his waistcoat.

"Nothing can be done. I'm sorry," said the vet.

Busto rebuttoned his waistcoat. "So what you wanna do? Killum?"

"It's the only merciful thing *to* do."

"How mucha dat cost?"

"Mmmmm, five shillings."

"But make 'im oright, dat aina possible?"

"Quite impossible."

"Not for no money?"

"Not for all the money in the world."

"Hooh! Well, what you want?"

"For my visit? Oh, well, I'll say half a crown."

"Go 'way," said Busto, poking half a crown at him.

"The dog will only suffer if you let him live on like this. I really——"

"I give-a you money for cure. For killum? No."

"I'll do it for nothing, then. I can't see the dog suffering——"

"You go 'way. Dissa *my* dog, hah? *I* killum! You go 'way, hah?" He approached the vet with such menace that the poor man backed out of the room. Busto poured another cup of red Lisbon, and drained it at once. "You!" he shouted to me, "Drink! . . . You, Mick! Drink!"

The wizened man helped himself to wine. Busto fumbled under one of the pillows on the bed, very gently in order not to disturb the dog, and dragged out a huge old French revolver.

"Hey!" I said. "What are you going to do?"

"Killum," said Busto. He patted the dog's head; then, with a set face, stooped and put the muzzle of the revolver to Ouif's ear. With clenched teeth and contracted stomach-muscles, I waited for the explosion. But Busto lowered his weapon; thought for a moment, rose and swung round, all in the same movement, confronting the lithograph of Mona Lisa.

"Twenna-five quid ada Convent!" he shouted.

Mona Lisa still smiled inscrutably.

"Fifty!" cried Busto. He returned to the table, poured three more drinks, and emptied another cup. Nobody spoke. Fifteen minutes passed. Ouif, brought back to consciousness by pain, began to whine.

"No good," said Busto. He clenched his teeth and again aimed at the dog's head. "Gooda dog, hah? Lil Ouif, hmm?"

He pressed the trigger. There was a sharp click, nothing more. The revolver had misfired. The dog whined louder.

"I knoo a bloke," said Mick, "a bloke what made money during the War aht o' profiteerin' on grub. Done everybody aht of every-fink, 'e did. So 'e 'as to live; this 'ere dawg 'as to die."

The walls of the room seemed to be undulating in a pale mist; the wine burned my throat. Busto opened a third bottle, drank, and returned to the bed.

"You look aht you don't spoil that there piller," said Mick, "if you get what I mean."

I shut my eyes tight. Out of a rickety, vinous darkness, there came again the brief click of the hammer on the second cartridge.

"Now, agen," said Mick.

Click. . . . click. . . .

"For God's sake call that vet back, and let him——"

"You minda you biz-ness, hah?"

"It's 'is dawg. 'E's got a right to kill 'is own dawg, ain't 'e? Pro-vided 'e ain't cruel. Nah, go easy, Busto, go easy——"

I hunched myself together, with closed eyes.

Click, went the revolver.

"Last cartridge always goes orf," said Mick. "Try once agen. 'Old yer gun low-*er.* . . . Nah, *squeeeeeeze* yer trigger——"

I pushed my fingers into my ears and tensed every muscle. The wine had put a raw edge on my sensibilities. I shut my eyes again and waited. I heard nothing but the pulsing of blood in my head. My fingers in my ears felt cold. I thought of the revolver-muzzle, and shuddered. Time stopped. The room spun like a top about me and the red Lisbon wine, the lunatic's broth, drummed in my head like a boxer with a punching-ball—*Ta-ta-ta, ta-ta-ta, ta-ta-ta.*

I opened my eyes. Busto was still kneeling by the bed. The revolver, still unfired, remained poised in his hand; but Ouif had ceased to whimper. He lay motionless, the petrified ruins of a dog.

"Anyway 'e die," said Busto.

"Of 'is own accord," said Mick. "Bleedn war-profiteers is still alive. So 'e 'as to die, if yer see what I mean."

"Some people complain," I said, "because men die and dogs go on living."

Busto made an unpleasant noise, with his tongue between his lips: "*Pthut!* Men is rubbish. Dogs is good."

He drank the last of the wine. Then, pensively raising the revolver, he cocked it and let the hammer fall. The last cartridge exploded with the crash of a cannon; the big bullet smacked into the ceiling, bringing down an avalanche of plaster; the revolver, loosely held, was plucked out of Busto's hand by the recoil and fell with a tremendous clatter and jingle of broken crockery among the teacups. For a moment we all sat still, stunned with shock. The clean piercing smell of burnt gunpowder cut through the close atmosphere of the underground bedroom. Busto jumped to his feet, kicked over the table, jerked his elbows sideways in an indescribably violent gesture and, raising his fists to the ceiling, yelled:

"Ah, you! Death! Greedy pig! Wasn't you a-belly full yet?"

Then he grew calm. He pointed to the body of Ouif and said to Mick: "Chucka disaway."

"Where?"

"Dussbin."

"Wot, ain't yer goin' to *bury* 'im?"

"Whagood dat do?" Busto turned to me, and made a familiar gesture. Raising his eyebrows and sticking out his chin, he pointed with the index finger of his left hand to the palm of his right, and uttered one sound:

"Hah?"

I remembered; paid him my rent, nine shillings and sixpence, and went up the creaking stairs to bed.

I should say, I suppose, that there was a great deal of good in Pio Busto—that a man who could love his dog must have something fine and generous somewhere in his soul. It may be so, but I doubt it. I said I feared him. That was because he was my landlord, and I had no money and knew that if I failed to pay my rent on Saturday I should be in the street on Sunday as surely as dawn follows night. How I detested him for his avarice, his greed, his little meannesses with soap, paint, and matches! Yet I admit that I felt a queer qualm of pity for him—that grimy, grasping, hateful little man—when he gave away cups of lizzie wine that night in the wash-house when the little dog Ouif lay dying in his bed. I don't know . . . there are men whom one hates until a certain moment when one sees, through a chink in their armor, the writhing of something nailed down and in torment.

I have met many men who inspired me with much more loathing than Busto, several of whom passed as jolly good fellows. It is terrible to think that, after the worst man you know, there must always be somebody still worse.

Then who is the last man?

The same applies to places. The insects at Busto's drove me mad. But, say I had been at Fort Flea? You will not have heard the story of Fort Flea, for it was hushed up. I got it from a man who learned the facts through an account written by a Mr. de Pereyra, who knew the commanding officer. It went into the official reports under the heading of *Fuerte di Pulce*, I think.

During the Spanish campaign in North Africa, in the latter years of the Great War, a company of Spanish soldiers occupied a fort. There was the merest handful of Spaniards, surrounded by at least two thousand Kabyles. Yet the tribesmen retreated and let them take the fort. Later, a Kabyle, carrying a flag of truce, approached the soldiers and, screaming with laughter, cried: "Scratch! Scratch! Scratch!" They didn't know what he meant, but they found out before the day was over.

The doctor, who had been attending two men who had been wounded, came to the captain and, in a trembling voice, asked him to come to the improvised hospital. "Look," he said. The wounded men were black with fleas—millions of fleas, attracted by the smell of fresh blood. They were coming in dense clouds, even rising out of the earth—countless trillions of fleas, which had their origins in a vast sewage-ditch which, for centuries, had received the filth of the town. They were mad with hunger; attacked everybody, swarming inches deep; drew points of blood from every man; killed the wounded, devitalized the rest, made eating impossible by pouring into the food as soon as it was uncovered, prevented sleep, made life intolerable. And nothing could be done. The Spaniards had the strictest orders to hold their position. A desperate dispatch was rushed to the general—General Sanjurjo, I believe—who sent a scathing reply. What kind of men were these, he wondered, who could let themselves be driven back by the commonest of vermin? So at last, when reinforcements arrived, there were only twelve men left, all wrecks. The Kabyles hadn't attacked: they had stood by, enjoying the fun. The rest of the men had been eaten alive; nibbled to death.

And I complained of the polite little insects in the bedrooms at Busto's.

THE APE AND THE MYSTERY

W HILE the young duke had been talking, the aged Leonardo had been drawing diagrams with a silver point on a yellow tablet. At last the duke said: "You have not been listening to me."

"I beg your pardon, Magnificence. There was no need. Everything is clear. Your water down there near Abruzzi is turbid and full of bad things, evil humors. Cleanse it, and this flux will pass."

"What," said the duke, "I must wash my water?"

"You must wash your water," said Leonardo.

The young duke stared at him, but he continued still drawing on his tablet: "You must wash your water. Tell your coopers to make a barrel, a vast barrel, as large as this hall, and as high. Now in this barrel you must lay first, clean sand to the height of a man. Then charcoal to the height of a man. Above this, to the height of a man, gravel. Then, to the top, small stones. Now down here, where the sand is, there must be a pipe. The bottom of this great cask will incline at a certain angle. The pipe will be about as large as a man's arm, but a plate of copper, or brass, suitably perforated, will cover the end embedded in the sand and will be further protected by a perforated case so that it may be withdrawn, if choked with sand, and replaced without considerable loss of pure water."

"What pure water?" asked the young duke.

"The pure water of Abruzzi, Magnificence. It will pour in foul at the top and come out clean at the bottom. These fluxes are born of the turbidity of the water."

"It is true that our water is far from clear."

"The purer the water, the smaller the flux. Now your water poured in at the top will purify itself in its downward descent. The greater pebbles will catch the larger particles floating in it. The smaller pebbles will take, in their closer cohesion, the lesser particles. The gravel will retain what the little pebbles let pass. The charcoal will arrest still tinier pollutions, so that at last the water—having completely purged itself in the lowest layer of sand—will come out pure and sweet. Oxen, or men (whichever you have most of) may pump the water by day and by night into my filter. Even your black pond water, poured in here, would come out clear as crystal."

"I *will* do that," said the young duke, with enthusiasm. "The coopers shall go to work, the rogues. This moment!"

"Not so fast, Magnificence. Let us consider. Where is the cooper that could make such a cask? Where is the tree that could yield such a stave for such a cask? Big pebbles, little pebbles, gravel, charcoal, sand. . . . Yes, reinforce it at the bottom and construct it in the form of a truncated cone. Still, it crushes itself and bursts itself asunder by its own weight. No, Magnificence. Stone is the word. This must be made of stone. And"—said Leonardo, smearing away a design on his tablet and replacing it with another—"between every layer, a grill. To every grill, certain doors. Bronze doors. The grills, also, should be of bronze. As for the pipes—they had better be bronze. A valve to control the flow of the water, a brass valve. Below, a tank. Yes, I have it! We erect this upon . . . let me see . . . fourteen stone columns twenty feet high, so that, since water must always run down to level itself, it would be necessary for your servants only to turn a screw, to open a spring of pure water, gushing out of a bronze pipe in twenty places at once in your palace, as long as the tank is full. I have also an excellent idea for a screw, designed to shut off the water entirely or let it in as you will, wherever you will, either in a torrent or in a jet no thicker than a hair's breadth. In this case, of course, your Magnificence will need a more powerful pumping engine. . . ."

The young duke asked: "What do you want all those bronze doors for?"

Leonardo said: "Magnificence, you have seen the pebbles in a stream."

"Naturally."

"You have seen them, and you have touched them no doubt?"

"Well?"

"They are slimy, are they not? They are covered with little green plants, you will have observed?"

"Well, well?"

"So will be the big pebbles, little pebbles, gravel, charcoal and above all the sand in your Magnificence's filter. Slime and green stuff will choke it, or make it a source of even more noxious water than ever before. Hence, the bronze doors. Every month the stones, charcoal, sand and so forth, are raked out and the empty places refilled with fresh stuff."

The young duke did not know what to say. He was uneasy. Turning an enormous seal on the forefinger of his right hand he muttered: "This is all very well. I have the greatest respect for your knowledge, and all that. But . . . stone, bronze doors, bronze gratings . . . I mean to say, bronze pipes, and God-knows-what made out of brass. You know all about these things, of course. But seriously, I really think we'd better let it drop. . . ."

"If you liked the pipes could be simply lead. The gratings would have to be copper, of course, but in about thirty or forty years . . ."

"Thirty or forty years!"

"What is thirty or forty years?" asked Leonardo, with a smile, combing his great beard with his fingers. "If you build, build for ever. Long after you are dead, Magnificence, by what will you be remembered? The fight you fought with Colonna? The bad portrait of you which you hired poor little Ercole to paint? Oho, no, no, no! Your descendants will say: 'Ah, that was the duke who washed the water here in Abruzzi and cured his people of their belly-aches.' Therefore I say stone of the hardest and bronze of the toughest. I know, Magnificence; I know."

"You know everything, Leonardo."

"I know a little of everything, and not much of anything—with the possible exception of the art of painting. Of that I know something. Yes, I know a certain something about painting pictures. But what is that worth? Little, Magnificence—so little! Your wall, upon which I smear my blood and tears, will fall. The bit of wood that I give my life to cover with pigments will warp, Magnificence, crack and rot. I grind my colors and I refine and refine my oils, and hope and hope for a few years more of life, as Leonardo da Vinci, when I have gone where I belong. But mark my words! One cup of sweet water out of your river down at Abruzzi—one cup of water, pure water, in the belly of a grateful ploughman—will make you immortal, and you will be remembered long after my colors fade. Simply because of a cup of clean water, Magnificence! So I talk in terms of hewn stone and mighty bronze, thinking of that cup of good water."

The duke found his opportunity to change this subject. "Ah, yes," he said. "Now that you mention it. Speaking of colors, and what not. You are the man who painted that picture of the Madonna Lisa, are you not? I mean the wife of Francesco di Bartolommeo di Zanobi del Giocondo—that one. Yes, of course you are."

"Yes," said Leonardo.

The duke said: "Remarkable man that you are! Today you make drains. Tomorrow you cast cannon. The day before yesterday you make a sort of Icarus machine, so that a man can fly like a bird. Ah . . . can you? Did it?"

"No, Magnificence, not yet."

"It would not surprise me if you could transmute metals. They say that you are something of an alchemist. Can you turn base metals into gold, Leonardo?"

"I have never tried."

"Try! try! Who knows? They tell me that the Valentinois has a learned doctor from the Lowlands who——"

"The tank," said Leonardo, making a diagram, "could be of copper, lined with——"

The duke said: "Yes, yes, yes, of course. Mona Lisa was a Neapolitan, or at least she was from the south. Yes, she was a Gherardini. Do you happen to know whether she was related to the Florentine family of that name?"

"No," said Leonardo da Vinci, "I know only that she married del Giocondo—he bought a picture of Saint Francis from Puligo. I have seen worse pictures. He is something of a connoisseur, Giocondo."

"I saw your picture," said the duke. "Between ourselves, it's not at all bad. La Gioconda is by no means a bad-looking woman. She's his third wife, you know."

"I know. Her predecessors were Camilla di Mariotto Ruccelai, and Tommasa di Mariotto Villana. They both died within four years."

"Ah, yes. There are some queer stories about that," said the duke.

"But to return to the tank, Magnificence."

"To the devil with the damned tank! Tell me, Leonardo—what was she always grinning about?"

"Madonna Lisa? She never grinned, Magnificence. She smiled, yes. Grinned, no."

"You must have been alone with her for a long time."

"Never for a moment," said Leonardo. "Never for one little moment. There were always waiting-women, secretaries, musicians, dress-makers, and frequently the lady's husband."

"A jealous man, that," said the duke.

"Yes. He is going the way to hell, as I nearly did, trying to find the bottom of a bottomless pit."

"She always struck me as deep," said the duke, "ever so deep—deep as the sea. D'you know what? She isn't by any means what you could call a beautiful woman. But, the few times I met her, I couldn't take my eyes off her. I am not," he said, curling the point of his red-blond beard between two fingers, "I am not altogether undesirable as far as women are concerned, and in any case . . . well, I should have . . . however, there was something about that woman that froze me. In a way, she frightened me. She never said anything. You know, I suppose, that if I want to be amusing—if I go out of my way to be sprightly and entertaining—I could make St. Bartholomew roar with laughter at the stake. Well, d'you know what? With the Madonna Lisa I had no success whatever. I believe you must have heard that I tell a tolerably good story. I told her three of the raciest and best I ever knew. There was never anything but that strange little pinched-up smile. You caught it perfectly, Leonardo. God knows how you did it, but you caught it. I stood and looked at the picture for nearly five minutes, and I said to myself: 'Aha—he has caught it. There is the smile. There she is. There is la Gioconda to the life. What is she smiling at? She might be the Mother of God or she might be the devil's wife.' And a sort of cold shiver went up and down my spine. Fortunately, at that time I was . . . anyway it was lucky for me that I had a certain other distraction just then. But one or two gentlemen I know completely lost their heads over her. Yet I am of the opinion—tell me what you think, Leonardo, because you have seen all the beautiful women in the world and know everything—in my opinion the Madonna Lisa is not beautiful."

"No."

"When you say 'no' Leonardo, do you mean 'no, she is not beautiful' or 'no, I disagree with you, she is beautiful'?"

"She is not beautiful," said Leonardo.

"It seemed to me that her hands were coarse and bony, but you painted them as if they had no bones in them. But she must have been an easy person to paint, because she moved less than anyone else I ever met in my life."

"Yes, nothing but the blinking of her eyes told you that she was alive," said Leonardo. "But sometimes she moved her hands. Occasionally she took her right hand from the back of her left hand, and loosely locked her fingers together. But generally she let her hands fall into her lap, where they lay relaxed, with the palms upwards. You see such a disposition of the hands in good old women who have done their work and are content to sit and look at their grandchildren. I have seen hands like hers on deathbeds— the deathbeds of women who have lived contentedly and died in peace with all their sins forgiven."

"Yes, she must have been easy to draw," said the duke. "She kept so still. Now if you were drawing me, Leonardo, that would be quite a different matter, because I can't keep still. I pick something up, I put something down, I walk here, I walk there, I take hold of a curtain or a piece of tapestry. . . ."

"On the contrary, Magnificence, that would make you all the easier to portray."

The duke, putting forward his right hand, said: "And what do you think of *my* hand?"

"It is a perfectly good hand," said Leonardo, without enthusiasm. "It will do everything you want it to do. I see by the third and fourth fingers that you are a horseman. The first and second fingers, and the thumb, tell me that you are a swordsman, and the tendons of your wrist tell the same story."

The duke said: "Her hands really were a little too large and hard. What made you draw them so round and soft?"

Leonardo replied: "I softened them to make a symbol of terrible strength."

"I saw no terrible strength," said the duke, "only pretty hands—pretty, soft, yielding hands."

Leonardo repeated: "Terrible strength. Soft and yielding. What is softer and more yielding than quicksand or a quagmire? And what is stronger? What is more terrible? In the sea, what is stronger and more terrible than those soft, yielding things that lie still in the dark and lay their pliable fingers, or tentacles, upon the diver?"

"I don't quite follow you," said the duke, "but, as I was saying, I could have fallen in love with that woman. I couldn't get to the bottom of her."

"You had better thank God that you did not fall in love with her, Magnificence," said Leonardo, "and as for getting to the bottom of her, that is impossible."

"Yes, as I said, the Madonna Lisa is deeper than the sea."

"No. She has no depth to which you could dive and no height to which you could climb. She is nothing at all. Del Giocondo will have discovered that much by now. She is, as you might say, God's judgment upon him, that poor devourer of women. He loves her insanely—and she smiles. He bites his fingers, beats his head against the wall, and goads himself into madness in his hopeless endeavor to find something in her that is tangible—something upon which he may lay his hand and say: 'At last I have found you.' And all the time she smiles, and is silent. He may fall on his knees and weep on her feet. She will smile. He may lock her in her chamber and starve her: she will smile. He may humiliate her, beat her with sticks, strike her before the servants . . . she will continue to smile. This I say with authority, because I have seen it all. And he knows that if he cut her throat, she would smile that enigmatic smile even in death . . . and he is exhausted, defeated. He is exasperated and worn out (just as I might have been) by his effort to know her."

"But you know her, Leonardo?"

"By the grace of God and an ape."

"How, an ape?"

Leonardo was tired of it all. He made a gesture like a man who is shaking water off his fingertips, and said: "Oh . . . like del Giocondo, like you, like a dozen others, I lost sleep thinking of her. The smile, the smile, the smile. I have seen every face in the world, from the throne to the gutter. I can read faces as your secretary can read a book. As a cut key fits the wards of a lock, so the shape of a face falls into position in a keyhole in my mind. Very good, this one baffled me," said Leonardo, laughing grimly. "I saw the agony of del Giocondo and the calm of the Madonna Lisa, and I wanted to *know*. I talked to her, watched her, employed ten thousand artifices to get her off her guard. And still she smiled. That smile came between me and my sleep. I hated her bitterly because she was too much with me. Then, to be brief, when the portrait was finished and my brushes put away, God sent the ape."

"What ape?"

Leonardo said: "Del Giocondo filled his house with musicians, tumblers, dancers, and all that, in order to amuse his wife. There was a choir of little boys that sang. There was a man who made me laugh—even me. Madonna sat with folded hands, quietly smiling. I finished the portrait. Then something happened. Del Giocondo had several large hounds. One of them, a buff-colored dog almost as big as a donkey, used to lie at her feet. This gigantic hound had hanging jowls and an expression of indescribable melancholy. When I showed the Madonna Lisa the finished picture, she nodded and said, through a pin-hole in her compressed mouth: "That is good." At this, the great dog, whose ears had caught some warmth in her voice, came forward lashing about with his great tail which disturbed a little sleepy ape no bigger than your two hands."

The duke looked at his hands.

Leonardo continued: "This absurd ape, enraged as little things are enraged, leapt upon the dog's back and pulled his ears, grimacing and chattering. The patient dog looked up with such absurd melancholy that it was impossible not to laugh. There was this gigantic dog, which might have killed a leopard," said Leonardo, half laughing at the memory of it, "and there was this preposterous ape chattering and chattering with ape-like anger while the dog feebly gesticulated with his tail, one friendly touch of which had been sufficient to knock his assailant head-over-heels. I laughed. Mona Lisa laughed—and then, by God, in the bursting of a bubble everything was clear. Then, Magnificence, I was a happy man, because I had uncovered a trivial truth, so that a thousand unconnected pieces fell together and made sense. La Gioconda threw back her head and opened her mouth and laughed, and then I knew why she had always smiled that strange quiet smile."

"Why?" asked the duke.

"She has very bad teeth, that vain and empty woman," said Leonardo, laughing, "but I have been thinking——"

"*Very* bad?" asked the duke.

"Rotten. Her smile is the secretive smile of a woman with bad teeth. Touching the matter of the water supply; I believe——"

"I detest women with bad teeth," said the duke, yawning. "And to the devil with your pipes and water-tanks."

THE KING WHO COLLECTED CLOCKS

Secrets such as Pommel told me burn holes in the pockets of the brain. If I could tell you the real name of the king and his country, your eyebrows would go up and your jaws would go down—and then, more likely than not, you would damn me for a sensational rogue and a dirty liar.

I met the Count de Pommel in the casino at Monte Estoril, in Portugal. At first I thought that he was a confidence trickster operating under a mask of shy reserve. The Count de Pommel had lost all his ready money on the third block of numbers, and was feverishly convinced that his luck was about to change. Offering me his watch as security, he asked me to lend him a thousand escudos; about ten pounds. In England, as things were then, almost any watch that ticked was worth ten pounds. I gave him the money. Then he began to win. In three-quarters of an hour he won eleven thousand escudos, stopped playing, and returned my money in exchange for his watch, with a thousand expressions of gratitude and the offer of a glass of champagne. He gave me, at the same time, six square inches of visiting card: he was the Count de Pommel, of the Quinta Pommel at Cascais and the Villa Pommel, Lausanne, Switzerland. The watch, he said, was worth four hundred pounds.

"Who made it?" I asked.

"I did," he said.

"There is something about you that made me think you were a clever man with your hands," I said.

He held out his hands. Transparent, bloodless, reticulated with narrow black veins, they seemed to vibrate like the wings of an insect. "Once upon a time, yes," he said. "Now, no. A nervous disorder. There is nothing worse than nerves in my profession."

"Your profession?"

"Or trade, if you prefer the word. I am, or was, a watchmaker. I got my title of nobility from King Nicolas, Nicolas the Third," he said, and added: "I am not a nobleman by birth. Actually, I was a Swiss."

"Oh, of course," I said, remembering. "Nicolas the Third collected clocks and watches."

"His was the finest collection in the world."

"And you—of course, of course! Pommel—now I get it— Pommel is a name I associate with the Nicolas clock."

The Count de Pommel smiled and said: "It was a toy rather than a clock in the proper sense of the word. Birds sprang out singing and flapping their wings, Father Time held up a mechanical calendar in the shape of an hourglass; and I devised a barometer also worked by clockwork, so that figures representing the four seasons appeared according to changes of atmospheric pressure. The Nicolas clock was overcomplicated. I am far more proud to have made the watch I pledged with you this evening."

"It seemed to me to be made of gold."

"Only the case. It is a very simple watch, but perfect; foolproof and waterproof—absolutely accurate. It seems silly, perhaps. I am a retired man, and time does not matter to me. Still, I like accuracy for the sake of accuracy—it is something to be achieved. I cannot work any more; my hands are unsteady, as you see. So I have a regard for that watch. It is the only thing left to me of all that I have made. The others are museum pieces, collectors' pieces—dead!"

"Did you also make the figures on the Nicolas clock, Count de Pommel? They are works of art."

"No, a Belgian artist made those: Honoré de Kock. We worked together."

"Ah, yes, Honoré de Kock. He died, didn't he?"

"Yes, poor Honoré. . . . He was a very good fellow. I liked him very much. It was a pity."

"He died in an accident, I believe?" I said.

"He died on purpose," said the Count de Pommel.

"You don't mean to say he killed himself?"

"No, far from it."

"Are you telling me that de Kock was murdered?" I asked.

"I would rather not talk about him just now, if you will excuse me."

"I beg your pardon, Count," I said.

He was troubled. "No," he insisted, "no, no, no! You have been very kind, very accommodating. I liked your face as soon as I saw you; and you were very good, too, charming! I should never have been so bold . . . only when I start playing, which is seldom, I am carried away. I take only a certain sum with me, and if I leave the table—then I lose the thread of the game. I can't imagine what possessed me to . . . to . . . to . . . Will you dine with us tomorrow, sir?"

"With pleasure," I said, and so we finished the bottle and parted; and I walked back to my hotel, thinking of incongruities. I remembered a temperamental plumber, a clumsy oaf with a soldering iron, who convinced everyone that he was a great craftsman because he was ferociously arrogant; and I thought of Pommel, the greatest living master of his craft, clock and watchmaker to King Nicolas himself—and singularly like a trapped mouse in his pitiful humbleness, in spite of his title of nobility.

I wanted to know more about him. Among other things, I wondered what sort of woman he had married. Pommel must have been more than seventy years old. I imagined a bloated, faded woman of fifty or so, soured by cumulative marital discontent.

I was wrong. She was fifty years old, and fat, but still attractive. Pommel called her Minna. Her hair was dull red, her eyes were blue and clear, and she had the warm, creamy, calm air of a woman who has achieved happiness, so that nothing can hurt or touch her. She was a Hungarian, and had been a needlewoman in King Nicolas's palace—the kind of girl that sings as she works and likes to sit still. She was well beloved, secure, healthy and contented—a woman who could grow festive over a crust, or dance to her own singing. Before an hour had passed I gathered that she had been poor Honoré de Kock's mistress, not because she liked him but because he was so unhappy; that she loved Pommel because he was happy with her and because he was kindhearted; and that there was a big, dark secret about which she had promised not to speak.

This, of course, was the inside story of the death of Nicolas, the king who collected clocks. In the end I got that story.

When I was twelve years old (said Pommel, after dinner) I was apprenticed to Tancred Dicker, and I learned a lot from him. You have, perhaps, seen pictures of him—Tancred Dicker, the one that looked like a sheepdog. Soon he let me work for him as a journeyman; I had the knack. By the time I was twenty I worked *with* Dicker. I went with him when King Nicolas asked him to come and stay and work on clocks, more than forty-five years ago, when I was twenty-two. When Dicker and I arrived we had first to meet a gentleman named Kobalt, a distant relation of King Nicolas's queen, a very powerful man indeed. The king relied upon him: the poor king was getting old, and had rheumatoid arthritis. He no longer cared very much for affairs of state, you see. He liked best of all his pastime, his hobby, which was collecting clocks and watches. Oh, yes, yes, the king had had other hobbies in his day; but he had got old—more than seventy-three years old—and turned his mind to higher things, being more or less tired out.

Before we saw the king we saw Kobalt, as I was saying, and Kobalt talked to us about what we had come for. You will have heard of Kobalt, no doubt—or it may be that he was a little before your time. It was Kobalt who ran away with Marli Martin, the wife of the minister; your father, more likely, heard of that affair. Kobalt is probably no longer in the land of the living; he must have been fifty years old when I first saw him more than forty years ago, and he was still good-looking. He was wicked, and a pig, but all the same he was a nobleman and a gentleman—a dangerous beast, and cunning; very brave—a wild boar, as you might say. He had light hair and moustaches, light-colored eyes, no eyelashes. As soon as I saw him I disliked him: there was badness all over him. He said to us:

"I am very happy to meet you. His Majesty is very anxious to consult with you. He is . . . but listen!"

He raised a finger, pulling out his watch with his free hand; smiled and said: "Exactly five o'clock." Almost before he had finished speaking, the place became full of music. Birds sang, bells rang, silver and golden gongs sounded—dozens and dozens of striking clocks chimed the hour. A German timepiece sent twelve lame-looking Apostles staggering out to strike a gold-headed Satan with bronze hammers. From a cheap wooden affair leapt a scraggy-looking little cuckoo with five hiccups, while a contraption under a glass dome let out five American-sounding twangs.

"His Majesty the King has a collection of more than seven hundred clocks," said Kobalt, as soon as he could make his voice heard. "He has a sort of weakness for clocks—like Louis XVI. But never mention Louis XVI in his Majesty's presence; the name of that unhappy monarch strikes a not-too-pleasant note in the king's ears. We'll see more of each other, I hope, my dear Monsieur Dicker. I am sure that we have much in common. Much!"

Dicker bowed low, and so did I. But I was full of a new idea. If his Majesty liked clocks, he should have clocks—toys, novelties, nonsense—clocks with figures and contrivances. That was when I first conceived the Nicolas clock. Tancred Dicker and I worked on it for four and a half years. Some of the technical innovations are his, but it was I who got the credit for the whole; and so I became watchmaker to King Nicolas III.

De Kock designed, modeled, and cast the case and the figures. He had talent—almost genius, the genius of the old Dutch Masters who could portray a man, an apple, a monkey, a grape, a bit of linen or a ray of sunshine, exactly as it appeared. He had a photographic hand; and it was this that made him unhappy— he wanted to make his own things, you see—it humiliated him merely to imitate the handiwork of the Lord God Almighty. He ate his heart out in his longing to create something with life of its own, but he never could. It is a sad thing when a man like de Kock becomes at last convinced that *au fond* he is a mediocrity; it breaks his heart.

Although he was very popular and successful and made a great deal of money, poor Honoré was very unhappy. He had already taken to drinking. Personally, I liked him very much indeed, and had a great admiration for him. He was a craftsman rather than an artist, he could work in any medium. Bronze, ivory, wood, marble, glass, gold, iron—anything and everything. Yet, because he could not reconcile himself to the fact that God did not see fit to give him the divine spark, he was always deep in melancholy. So it may, after all, have been true that poor Honoré de Kock committed suicide in the end. But I am by no means sure of this.

But where was I? Ay, yes, Dicker and I were talking to Kobalt, that smooth, terribly dangerous nobleman. It was a marvelous thing to hear all those clocks striking at once, and afterwards, when the last chime had died away (there was one vulgar little beast of a clock that was always a little late, and arrived breathless after all the others had done)—it was marvelous, afterwards, to listen to the ticking of all those clocks. The whole palace was full of it. At night, first of all, you could not sleep; you lay awake, listening, waiting for the concert that almost deafened you every quarter of an hour. There was one silly figurine of a dancing girl. Every hour she performed a little can-can, showing her underclothes, and kicking a tambourine which she held in her right hand. Another contraption—an old French novelty clock—was decorated with a dozen fantastic musicians. When their hour came they all went raving mad, throwing their limbs in all directions, while an extraordinarily strident musical box, concealed in their platform, played a lively jig. And there was a German clock—somehow a typically German clock—upon which there stood, in a painted farmyard, a farmer, his wife, his son, his daughter, and a pig. Without fail, twenty-four times a day, the farmer beat his wife, the wife smacked the son, the son kicked his sister, she pulled the pig's tail, and they all shrieked. A crazy clock! I could see that Dicker and I would have our hands pretty full, because these tricky toy clocks tend to be too sensitive, and sometimes have to be nursed like quarrelsome old invalids. What a business! His Majesty employed a staff of nine highly-skilled men who had nothing to do but wind up his clocks and see that they were set at the correct time. But he would not let them tamper with the works. That is what we had been employed for, at a salary that took even Dicker's breath away; and

Dicker was accustomed to eccentric millionaires to whom money was of no importance.

I am sorry. I am boring you with all this talk of clocks, clocks, clocks. But clocks, you see, are my whole life: I know nothing else. Also, if I am to tell you the really remarkable part of this story, I cannot avoid reference to clocks. His Majesty Nicolas III, in his old age, thought of nothing but his collection. You might have thought that a man, even a king, so old and broken (or, I should say, especially a king) would not like to be reminded of the passing of time. But no, his love of clocks was stronger even than his fear of death.

We were hurried to his presence. You might have thought that we were doctors and he was dying. Oh, dear me, how very old his Majesty was! He was sitting stiffly in a great velvet chair, wrapped from neck to ankles in a wonderful dressing-gown; and even with this, in spite of the fact that the windows were sealed and a fire was blazing, he seemed to be blue with cold. He was dried up, so to speak. There was no moisture left in him. Even his poor old eyes looked dry and he kept blinking as if he were trying to moisten them. The king was suffering from a sort of paralysis which, it was said, was the price he had to pay for certain youthful indiscretions. Also he had arthritis and moved with great difficulty, dragging his feet. I shall never forget how shocked I was when I first saw him. I had had some silly childish idea that a king in real life looks like a king. And there was this little, corpse-like man, old as the hills and weary of the world, quivering to the fingertips, shuddering and sighing and groaning, swaying his tired old head from side to side like a turtle. Only his beard was magnificent; it was like floss-silk, and covered most of his face and part of his chest.

But when he saw Dicker and me he came to life. He brushed aside the formalities and came straight to business. Oh, that awful voice! It was like a death-rattle, punctuated with groans. From time to time, forgetting his afflictions in his excitement, he started to make a gesture; but his arthritis stopped him with a painful jerk and he let out a moan of pain. He said that we were welcome, very welcome. We could have anything we liked, all we had to do was ask; even for money. We were to live in the palace, where a workshop had been fitted up. His clocks had been neglected. His beautiful collection of seven hundred rare clocks was going to the devil. We were to go to work at once. First and foremost, there was a job to be done on a unique Swiss clock. It had stopped. It was all the fault of one Fritz Harlin, who had poked his clumsy fingers into the works, pretending to repair it. This was to be put right at once, and he would watch while we worked. It was his only pleasure, that poor old king—watching workmen tinkering with clocks. He has sat and watched me for eight hours on end in my workshop; even taking his meals out of a vessel like a tea-pot—he could digest nothing but milk—on the spot.

We were conducted to this workshop, which was a workshop out of a dream. Upon the bench stood a silent clock upon which stood a bronze Father Time about two feet high, and a dozen other figures about four inches high. There was a king encrusted with jewels and wearing a golden crown; an enameled cardinal in a red robe; a knight in silver armor; a merchant carved out of lapis lazuli; a surgeon with a knife in one hand and a human heart made of a spinel ruby in the other; a nun of silver and ivory; an infanta of ivory and red gold; a painted harlot hung with odd-ments of jewelry; a peasant, all sinews, in old ivory and bronze; and an aged beggar made of bone and studded with sores which were little rubies. The idea was, at the striking of the hour, Time mowed these figures down, one by one, finishing with the king, who came under the scythe on the last stroke of midnight. It was a beautiful piece of workmanship, and we approached it with reverence.

Soon the King came in between two attendants. One of these was an old doctor and the other was a sturdy young man with a nondescript face; they supported him under the arms and led him to another red velvet chair. When Dicker and I began to bow the king said: "No, no, no need, no need. Get on with the work." Then, trying to make an imperious gesture with his hand, he cried out in agony and groaned with terrible oaths and curses. Dicker and I went to work. This Fritz must have been a fool. I will not try your patience with technical details; but he had not seen one dazzlingly simple thing—one steel wire, less than half an inch long, bent at an angle of about sixty-five degrees, upon which the movement of the main figures, and therefore the movement of the whole mechanism, ultimately depended. Wear and tear and tiredness— for even steel gets tired—had reduced this angle by half a degree. I adjusted it in thirty seconds with a pair of pliers, wound and set the clock, and then—swish went the scythe, down went peasant, soldier, priest and king while the clock was still solemnly chiming (it had little golden bells like church bells). His Majesty uttered a cry of delight, a groan of anguish, half a dozen shocking words and a gracious compliment. We explained that it was nothing; that we would make a new angle-pin of the finest tempered steel, and Time would cut down men for another hundred years.

And after that, I can assure you, Dicker and I were established, under King Nicolas III. We could do no wrong. I really believe that even if Dicker and I had committed murder it would some-how have been hushed up and we could have got away with it. Poor Dicker—this went to his head. Once, for example, when the chamberlain at the palace, a terribly proud man with a very hasty temper, told Dicker to remember his place, Dicker threatened to go home. The chamberlain was dismissed with ignominy.

This man, whose name was Tancredy, then conceived a frightful hate for the king, and secretly gave his support to the Liberal-Democrat Party. I dare say you will have read something about the political situation in that country in King Nicolas's time, especially towards the end of his reign when there was a great deal of discontent. King Nicolas, like his fathers before him, was an absolute monarch. In effect he was the Law.

After his father, King Vindex II, had been assassinated by a woman who threw a seven-pound bomb into his carriage, Nico-las, influenced by a wise old minister, had brought about certain reforms in the country. He had started a system of free education, free medical services, sanitation, the encouragement of the fine arts and of heavy industry, the development of an export trade—all this and much more was associated with Nicolas III. Nevertheless, the ordinary man of the people was subject to restrictions which horrified me. I am Swiss, you see.

There was no real freedom of speech or of the press. The average man had to glance over his shoulder before he felt it was safe to say what he wanted to say. There was frightful corruption in the highest places—especially when the king had grown too old and feeble and sick to care about anything but his seven hundred fantastic clocks. Consequently discontent was driven out of sight as an acorn is driven into the ground by your foot when you tread on it. This acorn, if I may put it that way, sent out all sorts of underground roots and pushed up unforeseen shoots. There were the Anarcho-Liberals, the terrorists of the Brutus party; the Democratic-Socialists, the Independent-Anarchists; the Republicans; the Labor-Royalists; and a dozen others. But the most subtle and formidable force working against the king was that of the Liberal-Democrat party, led by an ex-lawyer named Martin. This was a party to be reckoned with. Its methods were unquestionably constitutional and its policy was not to dethrone the king but to take away his power—which meant that the king would become a mere puppet; a king in name only. The Monarchists, who kept a great deal of personal power mainly because the king was a proper king, hated these Liberal-Democrats; and had indeed, my dear sir, very good reason to hate them. They were afraid of the Liberal-Democrats and of Martin, whose party was growing stronger and stronger. He was suspected of encouraging, and even of financing and inspiring, all kinds of anti-Nicolas propaganda—mysterious little newspapers, scurrilous and filthy books and pamphlets and cartoons printed abroad; riots, acts of terror, and sometimes strikes. But nothing could be proved. Martin was too clever.

It was believed that only the personality of King Nicolas III kept the system in one piece. And poor King Nicolas was senile, paralytic, crippled with arthritis, and not far from death. After he died—and he was expected to die fairly soon—all the quiet, pale things underground would rush out and overwhelm the country.

As long as the old king lived, the Monarchists had something to stand on. You see, nobody was allowed to forget that old King

Nicolas had been a much better man than his ancestors; that he was a humane, kind-hearted father of his people, and meant to make everyone happy as soon as he could afford to do so. Also, he was the king; as such, he inspired the people with an almost superstitious veneration.

But he had no issue. There had been only one son, a pitiful, sickly boy, who was dead of anemia.

It took me many months to learn all this, and, having learned it, I began to feel that, after all, Dicker and I were not as well provided for as we had thought.

By then I was working on the great clock of Nicolas. The old king came every day to watch while we worked. It is a strange thing: although I like a clock to be a clock and not a silly mechanical toy, I developed a kind of weakness for these ingenious little bits of machinery. It was very pleasant working in the palace: everything was to hand. His Majesty had a passion for exclusiveness: he insisted that the inner workings of the clock we were making should be seen by himself, Dicker, and (of course) me. Honoré de Kock worked with us later, because he, as the sculptor and caster of the figures, had to know what made them work. There was not a great deal for de Kock to do in the beginning. He was a bored, melancholy man, as I have said; and he could not keep his hands still; he was always playing with something.

One day, when it was necessary for him to stand by until we had worked out the details of the knee-joint of the central figure of the great clock of Nicolas, he began to knead and fidget with a large lump of putty on the bench. An hour passed. "What's that?" asked his Majesty.

"Nothing your Majesty," said de Kock.

"Show me," said the king.

Then we saw that Honoré de Kock with his fidgety, photographic hands had squeezed, gouged, and patted out of that lump of putty an exact likeness of Dicker. The King was childishly delighted and said: "Do one of me."

Poor de Kock bowed and said: "With pleasure, your Majesty, but not in putty. Putty will not hold its shape. If it would please you I could make your likeness in, say, wax—simply, Sire, as a little game to divert you."

Although it was early in the day, de Kock had already drunk a whole bottle of apricot brandy, and scarcely knew, or cared, what he was saying.

"Yes," he went on, "it might amuse your Majesty. One of the first commissions I ever had was a lady who had her likeness made in wax—full-length."

"What for?" asked the king.

"Why, her husband was suspicious of her, you see, because she was very much younger than he. She used to leave her room stealthily in the dead of night to visit someone else. Her husband was in the habit of peeping in at odd hours to see if she was still there. I made her a perfect likeness, movable at the joints like a dressmaker's dummy, so that she could put herself into all kinds of attitudes; and deceived her husband perfectly for three years."

"And what happened then?"

"Your Majesty, one night the husband crept in to spy upon his wife as usual, and was so overcome by the beauty of my waxwork that he ventured to creep up and kiss it. And then he rushed out yelling that his wife was dead—just as she came creeping back along the passage."

"And then? Did he kill her?"

"No, he broke up the wax model."

That was the only occasion on which I ever saw the king laugh. It hurt him, and the laugh turned into a groan, and the groan into a curse. But de Kock's story had put him into a very good humor. King Nicolas had been a very gay fellow in his time, fond of practical jokes—you know, making fools of people; pouring water over them, setting booby-traps so that when they opened the door a pailful of something nasty emptied itself over them . . . and so forth.

"Yes," he said to de Kock, "you shall make me in wax, life-size. But you mustn't tell anyone about it, do you hear? You go on and model me—every hair, every line, everything. Then we'll have fun. Yes, we'll play tricks. I shall be in two places at the same time. I'll frighten them out of their wits, the rogues. . . ."

Later, the king sent de Kock a beautiful gold cigar-case, studded with diamonds, but de Kock was gloomy and furious. "Why did I tell him?" he cried. "Why in God's name? After all these years—have I come down to making wax dolls for old men in their second childhood?"

But I said: "Wax doll or bronze doll, what is the difference? If it pleases the old gentleman, let him have it. You know how generous he is when he is pleased. You'll have to hang about in the workshop for several months, perhaps. You will be bored. Instead of playing with a bit of putty, play with a bit of wax, and do yourself some good at the same time."

De Kock was mollified; and set up a great lump of clay on a stand and went to work on the king's head. His technique was, if I remember rightly, as follows: first he modeled the head with microscopic accuracy in sculptor's clay. When this was dry, he made with infinite care a plaster mold, into which a special sort of wax was poured. So, the mold being taken away, section by section, like pieces of a jigsaw puzzle, out came the head, looking so horrible that it gave me a nightmare. It did not look a bit like the king at that stage, because de Kock had made him without the hair and the beard.

The putting in of the king's hair was the most tedious part of the business, because in a real life-like waxwork image every hair must be put in separately. I should not have cared for the job of putting in King Nicolas's beard a hair at a time; but when de Kock was at work he was a fanatic in his thoroughness. That is why he was what he was, poor fellow. Also, in spite of his first angry reluctance, he became engrossed in the king's head. He went to a shop where such things were sold, and bought an enormous quantity of beautiful silky white hair. (The starving peasant women of the Balkans, some of whom have beautiful heads of hair, sell their crowning glory for a few copper coins in order to buy something to eat.) The old king watched, blinking, fascinated. Then, looking at him, an idea occurred to me. I said to de Kock: "Since the old gentleman has taken such an interest in this doll, as you call it, why not let us combine our two arts? If you can fix your model constructionally, I can undertake to do the rest."

"What do you mean?" asked de Kock.

"Why," I said, "it would be no trouble at all for me to devise a clockwork mechanism to make him blink his eyes, sway his poor old head, tremble all over, and move those stiff, shaky hands of his. To me, that would be as easy as making a cuckoo-clock."

De Kock was delighted with the idea. We arranged it between us secretly, so as to give his Majesty a pleasant little surprise. If he wanted his harmless fun, he could have it. No one knew what we were doing. Dicker was very ill with a disease of the heart—of which, by the way, he died shortly after. So de Kock and I spent all our spare time playing with his dummy and, as a matter of fact, we really began to take quite a fancy to it—as a job, I mean. It had taken hold of us.

The machinery that made the eyes and the head move and the hands tremble was nothing: a mere toy-maker's job. I always liked difficult, intricate pieces of work. So it occurred to me that it might be really amusing to fix the jointed figure so that it could stand up and even take a few stiff rheumaticky paces backwards and forwards. That also was easy—hawkers in the street sell tin toys which can do that very thing; and even turn somersaults. No, it was not complicated enough for me.

Having made the dummy tremble and blink and sit and stand and walk, I now wanted to make it talk.

Well, you know that the phonograph had been invented then, although it was a very crude affair and did not sound real. But then again, neither did the king's voice sound real—in fact it sounded rather like a scratchy old phonograph record. Also, the king's voice was the easiest thing in the world for any man to imitate. You can imitate it yourself if you like. Let a lot of saliva run to the back of your throat and groan—there is the king's voice. I say once again, it was easy. The entire mechanism fitted into the back of the figure between the shoulder blades and the hips, and was operated by several levers. If you pressed one, the figure stood up. If you pressed another, it walked twelve paces forward and turned on its heel. So if you wanted the figure to pace up and down all you had to do was repeat the pressure on that lever.

Another lever made it sit down. As the thighs and legs made an angle of ninety degrees, the phonograph automatically started. Choking imprecations, together with groans of pain came out of the mouth. All the time the dummy shook and quivered, while a perfectly simple, concertina-shaped bellows inside the head sucked in the air and blew it out, so that the moustache that concealed the mouth was constantly in motion, and you could hear a kind of wheezy breathing.

It was all quite life-like, especially when we dressed it in clothes which we borrowed from the king's wardrobe. As the king's clockmaker, I was a person of great consequence in the palace. Everybody knew what had happened to Tancredy; they all went out of their way to be polite to me. I could even have had intrigues with duchesses if I had been so disposed. I had no difficulty in getting from the master of the king's wardrobe a complete outfit of the royal clothes, including fur slippers, a sable dressing-gown and a round velvet cap such as his Majesty invariably wore. When the dummy was dressed we sat it in a deep red velvet chair in the workshop, covered it with a sheet, and waited. At last the moment came. De Kock and I were excited, like children who have prepared a wonderful surprise for a beloved parent and are impatient to reveal it.

The king came in, with his doctor and his attendant holding him up, and was lowered, groaning and cursing, into his usual chair.

"What have you got there?" he asked.

I said: "A little surprise for your Majesty." Then I pressed two of the levers and whisked away the sheet all in one movement, and the dummy got up, walked twelve paces, which brought it face to face with his Majesty, and turned scornfully on its heel. I had measured my distance. Following it, I pressed another lever and it walked straight back to the chair and turned on its heel again. Another touch and it sat down, and the gramophone started and the great groaning voice bellowed dirty language right into the king's face.

I looked towards him laughing in anticipation of his delight, but what I saw horrified me. His face had become blue. His eyes seemed to be trying to push themselves out of their sockets. His mouth opened, and he uttered a terrible rattling scream. I still hear that scream in my dreams.

"Your Majesty," I cried, "forgive me!"

But he did not hear me. He fell back, and seemed to shrink like a sack of flour ripped open with a knife; and the old doctor, with a face as blue and terrified as the old king's, felt his heart and stammered: "Oh, my God! Oh, my God! Oh, my God! He's dead—the king is dead!" And I remember that the sturdy attendant, bursting into tears, threw himself on his knees and cried: "Oh, your Majesty, your Majesty! Don't go without me! Take me with you! Oh, your Majesty!" He shouted this in a heartbroken voice, something like the howl of a dog in the night. Then I heard footsteps; the door opened. I saw Kobalt with a dozen others behind him. Kobalt naturally looked first towards the king's chair, and when he saw what was there, the blood ran out of his face. Yet he was a quick-thinking man, even at a moment like this. He swung round and shouted: "Back to your posts! God help the man I find in this corridor! Colonel of the guard, a double guard on the outer gates—no one leaves the palace!"

After that he slid into the workshop, shut the door, approached the royal chair and said: "Doctor Zerbin—is his Majesty——?"

"His Majesty is dead," said the doctor, with tears on his face. I felt that it was I who had killed the king and I said: "Your Highness, it was all well meant. His Majesty asked us, de Kock and me, to make a figure, for a joke. The king wanted to——"

Kobalt turned, quick as a snake, with murder in his eyes. But then he saw the figure in the chair and his mouth hung open. He looked from it to the dead king. You know how death changes people. His Majesty, poor man, was all shrunk and shriveled and blue, and looked somehow less than half as big as he had been five minutes before. The dummy, in every hair and every baggy pouch and wrinkle, was the image of the king as he had been when he was alive. Kobalt came slowly towards me. I never was a brave man, and loathe violence. I thought Kobalt was going to kill me, and all in a rush I said: "Don't be hasty! De Kock and I are perfectly innocent, I swear it. His Majesty wanted a waxwork figure just to play a trick. A figure . . . like this. . . ."

And I pressed levers. I made the wax image of Nicolas III stand up. It walked twelve rheumaticky paces, looked at the corpse of the king, turned on its heel, strode back, sat down groaning and trembling, and puffed at Kobalt all the vile words you have ever heard, in a voice like the voice of his Majesty. Then it was still, except for a swaying of the head and a continuous tremor. In a quiet place, of course, anyone could have heard the noise of the powerful clockwork that made it move. But in the palace of poor King Nicolas III, where there were more than seven hundred clocks, the noise of cogs, ratchets and pendulums was perpetually in everybody's ears; even the members of the kitchen staff when they were out imagined that they were still hearing the ticking of clocks.

Kobalt actually bowed to the image and started to say: "Your Majesty," but he stopped himself after the first syllable, and said: "How very remarkable!"

"It is only a doll," said de Kock, and there was a certain gratification mixed with the terror in his voice, "a wax doll, a mere nothing."

"It looks real enough," I said, pressing the levers again; whereupon the figure got up, stood, walked twelve paces, turned, walked back, sat, groaned with agony and damned our eyes. Kobalt touched its wax forehead and shuddered. He went over to the king and felt his hand. Then his keen eyes veiled themselves. I could see that he was thinking hard and fast. It was not difficult to guess what was in his mind; the end of the king was the end of Kobalt. He, too, was as good as dead.

Soon he looked at me and said: "You made this machinery, did you? I want to have a word with you. And you, Monsieur de Kock, you made this waxwork figure? For the moment it deceived me. You are a very talented man, Monsieur de Kock . . . and his Majesty collapsed on seeing your little work, gentlemen? Few artists live to boast of a thing like that."

If he had simply said: "Few artists can boast of a thing like that,"

I might not be here to tell you this story. But when he said *"live to boast,"* I knew that there was something wicked in his mind. I knew that I was in frightful danger. Poor de Kock was already beginning to swell up like a pigeon, rolling his eyes and pushing out his chest. Kobalt went to a speaking-tube and blew into it, and then he said: "Major Krim? . . . Come down here at once with four or five men upon whom you can rely." Turning to me he said: "When I give you the word, make that thing work again."

With an air of reverence—smiling now—he threw the sheet with which we had covered the dummy over the dead body of King Nicolas. Footsteps sounded. "Now!" said Kobalt to me and I pressed levers. Major Krim, a man with a scarred face, came in with four others. As they entered, the dummy got out of the chair and walked abstractedly a few paces while Kobalt, keeping a wicked eye on me, said: "His Majesty commands that Dr. Zerbin and the attendant Putzi be put under arrest instantly and kept *incommunicado.*"

The thunderstruck doctor and the grief-stunned attendant were taken away. As the door closed the unhappy Putzi began to weep again, looking back over his shoulder at the thing covered by the sheet.

"Oh, you may well cry, you scabby dog!" shouted Kobalt, and then the image sat down groaning and quivering with the inevitable asthmatic curses, and the door closed.

Kobalt opened it again very quickly and glanced outside; shut it again and locked it, and said to me: "What a very remarkable man you are, my dear M. Pommel, to make something like that. Why, it is almost—if I may say so without irreverence—almost like God breathing the breath of life into clay. How does it work?"

I have always been a timid and obliging man, but now—thank God—something prompted me to say: "Your Highness, that is my secret and I refuse to tell you."

Kobalt still smiled, but there was a stiffness in his smile and a brassy gleam in his eyes. He said: "Well, well, far be it from me to pry into your professional secrets—eh, M. de Kock? . . . How wonderful, how marvelous—how infinitely more important than the

death of kings, who are only human after all and come and go—
how very much more important is the work that makes a man live
for ever! To be a great artist—only that is worth while. Ah, M. de
Kock, M. de Kock, how I envy you!"

Poor foolish de Kock said: "Oh, a mere nothing."

He had been drinking plum brandy. His vanity was tickled. I
could not help thinking that if he had a tail he would wag it then.

"How *does* that work?" asked Kobalt, and the very intonation
of his voice was a gross flattery. I could not stop looking at the
body of the king under the sheet; but de Kock, full of pride, said:
"What do I know of such things? Your Highness, I am an artist—
an artist—not a maker of clockwork toys. Your Highness, I neither
know nor wish to know, nor have I the time to get to know, the
workings of an alarm clock."

In quite a different tone of voice, Kobalt then said: "Oh, I see."
And so he gave another order, and Major Krim conducted de Kock
to his suite, where, three weeks later, he was found with his brains
blown out and the muzzle of a pistol in his mouth. The verdict
was suicide: de Kock had emptied three bottles of a liqueur called
Gurika that day.

But that is not the point. As soon as the Major had led de Kock
out of the workshop, Kobalt began to talk to me.

Oh, that was a very remarkable and a very dangerous man! You
were asking me about de Kock, earlier in the evening, and I said
that I was not quite sure whether poor Honoré really committed
suicide. Well, thinking again, I am convinced that he did not. The
butt of the revolver was in his hand, the muzzle was in his mouth,
and his brains were on the wall. There was one peculiar aspect of
this suicide, as it was so called: the revolver was held in de Kock's
right hand, and I happened to know that he was left-handed. It
seems to me that he would have picked up his revolver with the
same hand that he used to pick up the tools of his trade. A man
dies, if he must, as he lives—by his best hand. And then again: Dr.
Zerbin and the attendant Putzi disappeared.

I beg your pardon, all this happened later. I was telling you that
when I was alone in the workshop with Kobalt, he talked to me.

He said that he would give me scores of thousands, together with the highest honors that man could receive, if I would communicate to him the secret of that unhappy dummy that de Kock and I had made to amuse the King who now crouched dead in his chair. I have always been timid but never a fool. I became calm, extremely calm, and I said:

"I think I see your point, your Highness. Without his Majesty, you are nothing. Naturally you want to be what you are and to save what you have—you want to be, as it were, the regent in everything but name. If the news of his Majesty's death reaches Tancredy, you are out. You may even have to run for your life, leaving many desirable things behind you. Yes," I said, "I believe that I can see to the back of your scheme. Once you are acquainted with the working of this doll, you will work it. King Nicolas III, the poor old gentleman, was the father of his country, with half a century of tradition behind him. As long as King Nicolas could show himself to the people, the monarchy was safe. And as long as the monarchy was safe, you were great. This dummy here looks so much like his unhappy Majesty that even you, at close quarters, were deceived for a moment. If the real king had not been sitting over there, you would never have known anything. I may go so far as to say that the figure de Kock made and I animated is even stronger than the king because it can stand up and walk of its own accord, which his Majesty could not; and say the same things in the same voice. It can even write his Majesty's signature."

This, in point of fact, was perfectly true. The arthritic fingers of the king had no suppleness left in them, so that he wrote with his arm. Keep your arm stiff, grip a pen between the thumb and the first finger of your right hand, write the name *Nicolas* and you will see what I mean. Like this:

I had saved this for a last surprise—God forgive me. To demonstrate the truth of what I was saying (for I felt that I was fighting for my life) I got an inked pen, put it between the fingers of the dummy, and squeezed the thumb inwards. Immediately, upon a piece of paper which I presented, the pen scratched out the royal signature, and then the fingers opened and the pen was tossed aside.

"I will not tell you as much as I know," I said, "because I know that if I do, I shall be a dead man. It is useless for you to pry into the inside workings of this dummy because you will never discover three very important things. Only I can tell you how the clockwork is wound. There are nine different springs, which must be tightened in their proper order. There are certain very perishable parts, and these must be constantly replaced. I warn you that you had better leave me alone."

I said all this out of the mad bravado of a very nervous man, you understand. Having finished, and feeling myself on the verge of hysterics, I picked up a bottle that de Kock had left on my bench, and gulped down a couple of mouthfuls of it.

"I don't suppose you know that I could make you talk," said Kobalt, in a voice that made me shudder.

In reply I told him the honest truth. I said: "I am sure you could. But please don't. I can't stand pain. Oh, it is not only that," I added, as I saw him beginning to smile, "I can't stand pain—that's perfectly true—but when I said I shouldn't do it if I were you, I meant to say that the things I handle are actually more delicate than feathers. You could make me talk easily—you could make me talk by threatening me only with your fist. But don't you see?—the things I would tell you to do need a certain sort of hand, a certain kind of skill, and the training of many years. You'd never be able to do what you made me tell you to do. And I couldn't do it myself because you would have thrown me out of gear. Honestly, your Highness, you'd better leave me alone."

Kobalt looked at me steadily and coldly for a long time and then said: "My dear Monsieur Pommel, heaven forbid that I should argue with an expert. You're the greatest man of your time in your profession or, for that matter, any other. Let it be exactly as you say. Let us be friends. You are a cleverer man even than I thought."

And so it happened, my friend, that the real King Nicolas III—God rest his soul—was secretly buried somewhere in the country, having been carried out of the palace in a wine cask, while the dummy made by de Kock and animated by me became a head of state. The news was given out that the old king, miraculously recovered, could walk again, with only one attendant. I was that attendant. I had to be with him, to wind him up, keep him in good repair and press the proper levers. Every day I took him down to the workshop and he sat while I went on with my work on the great clock of Nicolas, which—as all the world must know—I completed. Another artist took up work on the moving figures where de Kock had left off. That is why experts have observed certain discrepancies.

It is fantastic, when you come to think of it: I was the real ruler of that country. I was the hand, the voice, the presence and the personality of his Majesty, King Nicolas III! Kobalt continued to be a man of power. When he, in conjunction with the Minister of the Interior, put forward the Monopol bill that included clauses involving the oppression and persecution of Jews, I caused King Nicolas to run a wet pen across the document. He tossed away the pen with a groan and an oath, without signing. After that, the whole world marveled at the renewed vigor of this aged man.

At about this time, my dear Minna came into the story. I hate to say it, but old King Nicolas—like the aged King David in the scriptures—used to keep himself warm at night through the proximity of young women. I provided a young woman. His Majesty had always loved women of a certain shape with red hair. He said that their very presence kept him alive. It was necessary for me to have someone whom I could take into my confidence, because my nerves were giving way. Remember, all this went on for several years. My dear Minna kept company at night with the wax image of Nicolas III. I taught her how to work the levers that made it move, and cut for her a copy of the big key—it had a handle like a corkscrew—that went into the little hole in the region of the left kidney and wound him up. From the beginning there was a deep sympathy between us . . . was there not, Minna, my little love?

It was Minna, in fact, who made a nobleman of me. She said: "Why should you not call yourself by the same title as others do?" She was right. I was a foreigner, and not well born. People were talking. It was impossible for me to discuss things with the gentry as man-to-man. I procured a Patent of Nobility and, over the signature of his Majesty, became the Count de Pommel.

Meanwhile, I believe, I was instrumental in bringing about more reforms. We taxed the big landowners, we built big blocks of flats for workmen, we sent an expedition to observe weather conditions; we brought engineers from Scotland to improve the tramway system and installed electric light, and we did a great deal to establish the paper industry. We cultivated tobacco in the south and were beginning to draw revenue from exports. I had always wondered why the whole world had not heard of *aka*, the smoked roe of a fish that lived only in one of our lakes. *Aka* is delicious. We made a monopoly of it, salted it, bottled it, and sold it back to our own country and to the world.

If all had been well, I might have made an earthly paradise. But it was too good to last. All the intrigues of Kobalt, all the agitation of the Liberal-Democrats could not hurt us. The monarchy had never been stronger. No, it was the will of God. In the first place, the surface of de Kock's dummy began, naturally, to show signs of wear and tear. I could have adjusted that. I could have found another waxwork artist and kept him perpetually incarcerated. I could easily have done this. It was not a matter of the first importance. A thousand times more important than the appearance of his Majesty was, in the long run, the way he behaved. How he moved, and what he said, you understand, depended on me.

One morning I awoke out of an anxious dream and found that my hand was unsteady. Do not misunderstand me—mine was not a drunken tremor, because I never used to drink. It was anxiety, I think, that made me shake. It was extremely serious. Everything depended on my skill. I began to worry. And the more I worried, the more I trembled. I could easily, no doubt, have employed a highly skilled watchmaker, and trained him, telling him exactly what to do . . . keeping him in confinement, *incommunicado*. But I did not dare. Also my magnifying glass began to be misty, and the mist would not wipe off. To be brief, my eyes were going. A tremor and a foggy eye—that is death to a watchmaker.

Yet again, in spite of everything, in spite of all I had done, the Liberal-Democrats had got stronger under Tancredy. Trouble was brewing. Still, I should have stayed on to the end if Minna had not been there. Thank God, she made me see reason. Dear Minna said: "What is all this to you, Pommel, my dear? You are a Swiss. Most of your money is in the Bank of Lausanne. You can retire and do what you like. The great clock of Nicolas is finished. The old king died years ago. Be sensible and get out now!"

It seemed to me that Minna was right. I could no longer trust myself to work as I used to. I arranged for Minna and for me what the French call a *coupe-fil*, a "wire-cutter"—a diplomatic passport. Having plenty of money—my wages only, and no plunder—put away in Switzerland, I drove with Minna over the border, and so, after many years, came home.

A little later, I learned that Kobalt had led his Majesty to address a delegation of Liberal-Democrats. Kobalt pressed the wrong levers. His Majesty sat down, cursed abominably, got up, walked twelve paces—straight into the fire—and stood, his hair and clothes blazing. As he stood, he melted. The fire took hold of the wax. The burning wax ran over the thick carpet. One wing of the palace was burned down. After that, upon the slogan *The king is dead: long live the people*, the Liberal-Democrats scrambled up to power, and then were overthrown by the Communal-Workers' party. The Communal-Workers were later accused of having shot King Nicolas III in a cellar. Tancredy went into exile. The last time I heard of Kobalt, he was supposed to be running a very prosperous nightclub in one of the Latin-American countries . . . but I do not know anything about this, and I do not care to know. I cannot think of that man without a shudder.

But, on the whole, it is a strange story in its way—No? A little out of the ordinary—Yes?

BONE FOR DEBUNKERS

Oᴺ a blast of bitter east wind that rushed down Great Russell Street came a spatter of cold raindrops that bit like small shot. I reached the portico of the British Museum one jump ahead of the storm, and there, standing apart from the students who had come out of the reading room for air and sandwiches, illuminated by a lightning flash, stood Karmesin in a black rubber Inverness cape reaching to his ankles and an oilskin hat shaped like a gloxinia. One hand grasped a Kaffir knobkerrie with a gold-plated head, while the other applied motions as of artificial respiration to his half-drowned moustache, and he was glaring at a Polynesian monolith in such a manner that I half expected its great stone eyes to look uneasily away.

"Third storm this morning," I said. He looked at me, glowering like the Spirit of the Tempest.

"A wretched day would not be complete without you. I would invite you to offer me coffee, if I did not object to sitting at table with imbeciles," he muttered. "Do you realize I could sue you, your publishers and printers, your distributors, newsagents and booksellers for millions? And I would, too, if I needed petty cash. How dare you describe me as 'either the greatest criminal or the greatest liar the world has ever known'? This is libelous: a liar always betrays a desire to be believed. Damn your impudence, have I ever cared whether you believed me or not?"

"No," I said, "but——"

"No," he interrupted. "And you assume that a truly great criminal never talks of his work, but how wrong you are! A confession unsupported by evidence is only a story, and I leave no evidence. I run no risk in telling you certain incidents, you scribbler, to enable you to put a few greasy pennies in your moth-eaten pockets. Remember this: the most pitiful sucker on earth is your sceptic. If you insist, we will go to the Cheese Restaurant and have a bit of Brie and a glass of wine."

The rain abating, we went; but Karmesin was not easily to be placated this morning. He continued, "It's not so much your catch-phrases that annoy me as your writing; I read your version of how, having disguised myself as a statue in Westminster Abbey, I discovered a sonnet of Shakespeare in Spenser's tomb, and I blushed for you."

"All I did was——" I began, but Karmesin interjected, "You be quiet!" At least the cheese appeared to please him. "I like Brie and wine," he said.

"They are the two things in this world that are impossible to fake. Not even Melmoth Agnew could successfully counterfeit their flavor."

"Strange name," I said.

"Strange man," said Karmesin. "If only you could write, what a story you might tell about him and me—for without me, he is nothing—and about the Society for the Clarification of History." He shook his great head. "But I can just see you describing Melmoth Agnew, for instance, as 'an anaglyphic character'—here you put three dots—'a personality in low relief'—then more dots—'In other words, he had practically no individuality of his own.'"

I said, "Have more cheese. For goodness' sake, have some more wine. Have a cigarette."

He accepted gruffly and continued, "I had occasion just now to upbraid a certain inky little penny-a-liner not a hundred miles from here in connection with a sonnet of Shakespeare. Then, the name of Melmoth Agnew comes up in connection with cheese, and in spite of myself I find myself telling you that I once employed the fellow in a matter concerning quite a different kind of Shakespearean document."

I said, "What sort of document?"

"Ah, you are saying to yourself, 'Old Karmesin is going to tell me now that he discovered a lost play by that greatest of poets.' As usual, you are entirely wrong," he said, then told this story:

I employed Agnew when I felt morally bound to do a service for a distressed gentleman. Do you know what a gentleman is? A gentleman is one who, among other things, does not twist his friends' conversation into excruciating prose forms and hawk them from editor to editor (said Karmesin, giving me a hard look).

The gentleman we will call Sir Massey Joyce of King's Massey, in Kent. I had not seen him for a long time; nobody had. They said he had turned recluse and buried himself in the country. Having been abroad for some years I had lost touch with him. Then, one day, certain business taking me to Ashford, it occurred to me to drive over and say "How d'you do."

You have seen photographs of King's Massey in *Stately Homes of England*. It is a beautiful old house, in three different styles of architecture—early Tudor, part of it "modernized" by Inigo Jones in the 1620's, with a wing by Adam built in the eighteenth century—the incongruities oddly harmonious. Massey Joyce was confused, almost embarrassed. He said, "My dear fellow, come in! Come in!"

For a recluse, I thought, he was remarkably pleased to have company. "It's nearly dinner time," Massey said. "Let's have a glass of sherry," and the old butler, Hubbard, served us, while my host chattered of things past in London.

He is lonely, I said to myself as we went in to dinner. The great mahogany table was set sumptuously with the Joyce plate. The huge silver-gilt centerpiece was heaped with fresh fruit. Old Hubbard poured us a rare old Chablis and served a fish course—three tinned sardines. After this, the entrée came up: there was a profusion of garden vegetables and, on a gleaming silver platter, canned corned beef, thinly sliced. With this—Well, did you ever try bully beef with a vintage *Clos de Vougeot?* It's rather curious. And then there was a little block of pasteurized synthetic cheese with a bottle of rare old port, and some coffee-type essence in cups of Sèvres porcelain accompanied by a hundred-year-old brandy and superlative cigars.

After dinner, sitting over more brandy in the library, Massey Joyce said to me, "There's enough wine and cigars in the cellar and the cabinets to last out my time: I don't entertain much nowadays. But for the rest, one rubs along, what?"

I said, "It might appear, old friend, that things aren't all they should be."

He answered, "Confidentially, I'm stone broke. I say nothing of taxes. Certain domestic affairs, which we'll not discuss, set me back more than I had—over a quarter of a million. Everything you see, except the wine, the tobacco and these books, is entailed or mortgaged."

I said, "I know, Massey. Norway sardines and Argentine beef might be a quirk of taste; but never penny paraffin candles in silver-gilt sconces."

"Well, I can't bilk the fishmonger and the butcher," said he. "The books must go next."

I was shocked at this; Sir Massey Joyce's library was his haven, his last refuge. It was not that he was a bibliophile: He loved his library—the very presence of all those ranged volumes with their fine scent of old leather comforted him and soothed his soul.

He went on, "Anyway, this is a deuced expensive room to heat. I'll save insurance too. I'll read in the little study, where it's snug. Oh, I know what's in your mind, old boy. How much do I need, and all that, eh? Well, to see my way out with a clear conscience, I want ten thousand pounds. Borrowing is out of the question—I could never pay back."

I said, "Between old friends, Massey, is there nothing I can do for you?"

"Stay with me a day or two. There's a man coming about the library. I thought I might get more, selling by private treaty. He isn't a dealer; he's an agent for the Society for the Clarification of History. You know, ever since Boswell's diary was found in an old trunk, there's hardly an attic or a private collection in England they haven't pawed over. I'm told they have all the money in the world, and anything they want they'll pay a fancy price for. What the devil *is* this Society for the Clarification of History, anyway?"

I said, "You know how it is; a few people like to make something, but most people prefer to break something. You may earn a crust praising great men, but you will get rich belittling them. The Society for the Clarification of History is fundamentally a debunking society; it's just the kind of thing fidgety millionaires' widows like to play with.

"It's back-fence gossip on a cosmic scale. There's excitement in it and controversy in it and publicity; and it's less bourgeois than endowing orphanages—and not half as expensive. They like to prove all kinds of things—they are heritage busters and tradition wreckers: Paul Revere couldn't ride; Daniel Boone was a Bohun and, therefore, rightful king of England; the author of *Othello*, in certain lines addressed by the Moor to Iago, prophesied the great fire of Chicago. Touching which, their great ambition is to prove beyond doubt that Francis Bacon wrote the works of William Shakespeare. They'd give their eyeteeth for incontrovertible evidence of that."

"All poppycock!" Massey Joyce shouted. "Bacon did nothing of the sort."

"Drop it. I know he didn't. Why do you want me to stay?"

"I beg pardon, old fellow. That Baconian nonsense always irritates me. Apart from the joy it is to have you here, I want you with me because one of these Clarification of History people called Dr. Olaf Brod is coming Wednesday morning. You're shrewd. I'm not. Handle the business for me?"

I said I would and that he was not to worry; but my heart misgave me. True, Massey Joyce had 25,000 volumes, many of them rare, especially in the category of the drama. But books, when you want to buy them, are costly and, when you need to sell them, valueless. However much had been spent on the library, Massey Joyce would be very lucky to get a couple of thousand pounds for the lot.

I did not sleep well that night; the owls kept hooting *O Iago! . . . Iago . . . Iago. . . .*

I was concerned for my old friend; in times like these, we must preserve such honorable anachronisms as Sir Massey Joyce. He was one of the last of a fine old breed: a benevolent landlord, proud but sweet-natured and a great sportsman. He was the Horseman of the Shires, who had finished the course in the Grand National; at the Amateurs' Club he had fought eight rounds with Bob Fitzsimmons; as a cricketer he was one of the finest batsmen in the country; and he was a stubborn defender of individual liberty, a protector of the poor and third-best-dressed man in England. A Complete Man. And, furthermore, a patron of the arts, especially of the theatre—his first wife was Delia Yorke, a fine comic actress and a very beautiful woman in her day.

This marriage was perfectly happy. Delia was the good angel of the countryside. But they had a wretch of a son, and he went to the dogs—he drank, swindled, forged, embezzled and, to hush matters up, Massey Joyce paid. Having run down to the bottom of the gamut of larceny, the young scoundrel became a gossip columnist and then went out in a blaze of scandal, when a woman he was trying to blackmail shot him. This broke Delia's heart, and she died a year later.

But my dear friend Massey Joyce had to live on, and so he did, putting a brave front on it. Then he married again, because he met a girl who reminded him of his truly beloved Delia. She was much younger than Massey, also an actress, and her only resemblance to Delia was in her manner of speaking: she had studied it, of course. This was the best job of acting that shallow little performer ever did. Massey financed three plays for her. They were complete failures. She blamed Massey naturally, left him and ran off with a Rumanian film director.

Massey let her divorce him, saying, "That Rumanian won't last. Poor Alicia can't act, and she ain't the kind of beauty that mellows with age. She'll need to eat. It's my fault anyway. What business has an old man marrying a young woman? Serves me right."

Outwardly he looked the same, but he seemed to have lost interest. He sold his stable, rented his shooting, stopped coming up to town for the first nights, sold his house in Manchester Square, resigned from his clubs, locked up most of King's Massey and lived as I have described. I had not known he was so poor. Before dawn, giving up all hope of sleep, I carried my candle down to the library: the electricity had been cut off, of course.

A glance at the catalogue more than confirmed my misgivings, Readers of these kinds of books are becoming fewer and fewer; there was not a dealer in the country who would trouble to give Massey Joyce's treasure shelf space. Hoping against hope I opened a cabinet marked MSS: ELIZABETHAN. The drawers were full of trivial stuff, mostly contemporary fair copies, so-called, of plays and masques, written by clerks for the use of such leading actors as knew how to read.

My heart grew heavier and heavier. All this stuff was next door to worthless. The sun rose. Chicago, Chicago, Chicago! said a sparrow. And then I had an idea. I took out of the cabinet a tattered old promptbook of the tragedy of *Hamlet*, copied about 1614 and full of queer abbreviations and misspellings, and carried it up to my room. Although I knew the play by heart, I reread it with minute attention, then put the manuscript in my suitcase, and went down to breakfast.

Over this meal I said to Massey Joyce, "It's understood, now. I have a free hand to deal with this Dr. Olaf Brod and his Society for the Clarification of History?"

"Perfectly," he said, "I'm grateful. He might come out with some of that damned Baconian stuff, and I'd lose my temper."

"Just keep quiet," I said.

And it was as well that Massey Joyce did as I advised, for Olaf Brod was one of those melancholy Danes that rejoice only in being contradictory. His manner was curt and bristly, like his hair. He bustled in about lunchtime and said, in a peremptory voice, "I haf time now only for a cursory glance. I must go unexpectedly to Vales. Proof positif has been discovert at last of the nonexistence of King Artur. Today is the secondt of July. I return on der tventiet."

He rushed about the library. "I had been toldt of manuscripts," he said.

I replied, "Doctor, we had better leave those until you can study them."

"Yes," he said, "it is better soh." But he stopped for a quick luncheon. Massey had up some golden glory in the form of an old still champagne. Doctor Brod was severe. "I am a vechetarian," he said.

Massey asked, "Isn't wine a vegetable drink, sir?" With his mouth full of carrots, Brod replied, "Not soh! Dat bottle is a grafe-yard. Effery sip you take contains de putrefiedt corpses of a trillion bacteria of pfermentation."

"Hubbard, fresh water to Doctor Brod," said Massey, but Brod said, "Der vater here is full of chalk; it is poisonous. It makes stones in der kidleys."

Massey said, "Been drinking it sixty-five years, and I have no stones in my kidneys, sir."

Olaf Brod answered, "Vait and see. Also, der cigar you schmoke is a crematorium of stinking cherms and viruses." Luckily he was in a hurry to leave. But he paused on the threshold to say, "On de tventiet I come again. No more cigars, no more vine, eh? Soh! Boil der vater to precipitade de calcium. Farevell!"

I said to Massey Joyce, having calmed him down, "I'll be here on the nineteenth, old fellow."

He said, "There'll be murder done if you ain't!" Then I hurried back to town, taking that old promptbook copy of *Hamlet* with me. I also took a little lead from one of the old gutters in the Tudor part of King's Massey. What for? To make a pencil with, of course; and this was a matter of an hour. I simply rubbed the sliver of metal to as fine a point as it would conveniently take: it wrote dull gray. This done, I went to see Melmoth Agnew.

You would have loved to describe him; you would have pulled out all the stops (said Karmesin and, in a horrible mockery of my voice and style, he proceeded to improvise). Melmoth had pale, smooth cheeks. His large round eyes, shiny, protuberant and vague, were like bubbles full of smoke. The merest hint of a cinnamon-brown moustache emphasized the indecision of his upper lip. He carried his cigarette in a surreptitious way, hidden in a cupped hand. He had something of the air of a boy who has recently been at the doughnuts and is making matters worse by smoking. I half expected his black silk suit to give out a faint metallic crackle, like burnt paper cooling. His silk shantung shirt was of the tints of dust and twilight, and his dull red tie had an ashen bloom on it like that of a dying ember . . . That's your kind of writing, give or take a few "ineluctables" and "indescribables" and whatnot. Bah!

Agnew was a kind of sensitized Nobody. You have heard of that blind and witless pianist whom P. T. Barnum exhibited? The one who had only to hear a piece of music played once, and he could play it again, exactly reproducing the touch and the manner of the person who had played before him, whether that person was music teacher in a kindergarten or a Franz Liszt? Great executants deliberately made tiny mistakes in playing the most complicated fugues; Blind Tom, or whatever they called him, reproduced these errors too. Agnew was like that, only his talent was with the pen. He had only to look at a holograph, to reproduce it in such a manner that no two handwriting experts could ever agree as to its complete authenticity.

I had previously found several uses for Melmoth Agnew; this time I carried him off to the British Museum, where I made him study some manuscripts of Francis Bacon. This peculiar fellow simply had, in a manner of speaking, to click open the shutters of his eyes and expose himself for a few minutes to what he was told to memorize.

I warned him to take especial care, but he assured me in the most vapid drawl that ever man carried away from Oxford, "The holograph of Lord Verulam, Viscount St. Albans, is indelibly imprinted on my memory, sir. I am ready to transcribe in his calligraphy any document you place before me. Problems of ink, and so on, I leave to you."

"It is to be written with a lead point."

"Then it is child's play," said he, wanly smiling, "but it would be so much nicer in ink." I knew all about that. There are other experts who, with chemicals and spectroscopes and microscopes, could make child's play of detecting new from old, especially in mixtures like ink and the abrasions made by pens.

Against a coming emergency, which I was anticipating, I had in preparation an ink of copperas, or ferrous sulphate, which I made with unrefined sulphuric acid and iron pyrites; gum arabic out of the binding of a half-gutted Spanish edition of Lactantius dated 1611; and the excrescences raised by the cynips insect on the *Quercus infestoria*, better known as nutgalls—the whole adulterated with real Elizabethan soot out of one of the blocked up chimneys of King's Massey. But it would take a year to age this blend, and there was no time to spare. This was none of Agnew's business.

I showed him the promptbook copy of *Hamlet* and said, "Observe that the last half page is blank. Take that lead stylus and, precisely in Francis Bacon's hand, copy me this." I gave him a sheet of paper.

Having perused what I had written there, he said, "I beg pardon, but am I supposed to make sense of this?" I told him, "No. You are to make a hundred pounds out of it."

So Agnew nodded in slow motion and went to work, silent, incurious, perfect as a fine machine, and the calligraphy of Francis Bacon lived again. He was finished in half an hour.

"I'm afraid it's rather pale," he said apologetically.

I said, "I know. Forget it." And such was his nature that I believe he forgot the matter forthwith; he even had to make an effort to remember his hundred pounds—I had to remind him.

Now I will write out for you, in modern English, what I had given Agnew to copy. In this version, I will make certain modifications in spelling, so that the riddle I propounded conforms with the key to it. Here:

> *I seek in vain the Middle Sea to see,*
> *Without it I am not, yet here I be*
> *Lost, in a desperate Soliloquy.*
> *If you would learn this humble name of mine*
> *Take 3 and 16 and a score-and-9.*
> *Count 30, 31, and 46,*
> *Be sure your ciphers in their order mix,*
> *Thus, after 46 comes 47*
> *As surely as a sinner hopes for Heaven.*
> *Take 56, and 64 and 5,*
> *And so you will by diligence arrive*

At numbers 69 and 72.
Five figures running now must wait on you
As 86, 7, 8, 9, ten fall due,
'Tis nearly done. Now do not hesitate
To mark 100; 56, 7, 8,
My mask is dropt, my little game is o'er
And having read my name, you read no more.

Of course, this should not tax the intelligence of the average coal heaver, in possession of all the clues I have given. Yet, for you, I had better explain!

What desperate soliloquy in *Hamlet* contains the words, "No more?" The familiar one, of course: "To be, or not to be," and so on.

Examine that sombre opening to Hamlet's soliloquy; and you will notice that, curiously enough, the letter C does not occur anywhere in the first six lines. The writer is not a homesick Spaniard or Italian from the Mediterranean, which formerly was called the "Middle Sea." He refers to the missing C in his name. He has buried his identity in the first half dozen lines of Hamlet's familiar soliloquy.

Having guessed this far—why, babes in kindergarten solve trickier puzzles than this riddle of the rhyming numbers. Starting with "To be," count the letters by their numbers, as far as "No more." Letters *3, 16, 29, 30, 31, 46, 47, 56, 64, 65, 69, 72, 86, 87, 88, 89, 90, 156, 157* and *158*. So it reads:

> *To* B*e, or not to be*—th*A*t *is the questi*ON:
> W*hether 'tis noble*R I*n the mind* T*o suffer*
> TH*e sl*I*ng*S *and arrows of ou*TRAGE*ous fortune*
> *Or to take arms against a sea of troubles,*
> *And by opposing end them.* T*o* DIE—*to sleep*—
> *No more . . .*

Hence, "Ba-on writ this tragedie." Without his middle C, Bacon is not; yet here he is. And so he tells you, and in his own handwriting too!

A real lawyer's split-hair quibble, what? Just tortuous enough. A meaty bone for the debunkers, eh? It might be asked, "Why should Bacon have written this?" The answer is: "Bacon liked actors; he wrote it in a promptbook to amuse some sprightly player after a theatrical supper, circa 1615."

So, having suitably oxidized the faint lead in the pencil marks, half erasing them in a process of ever so gentle abrasion, I returned to King's Massey on the nineteenth and slipped the promptbook back where I had found it.

Massey Joyce said, "I do hope this Brod man coughs up. Do you know, Hubbard and his wife—who cooks and housekeeps—haven't had any wages for three years? I tried to pay 'em off when I sold my guns and sporting prints, but they wouldn't go. Begged pardon; said they'd known the good times, and by the Lord Harry they'd stand by in the bad."

"Do those Elizabethan manuscripts of yours mean much to you?" I asked.

He said, "No. Why?"

I told him, "Why then, Massey, we'll save your old books yet. Only you keep right out of it. Have a migraine; keep to your room and leave it to me."

So he did; and Doctor Brod turned up on the morning of the twentieth with a friend, one Doctor Brewster, also of the Society for the Clarification of History, but lean and keen, with a business-like dry-cleaned look about him. As I had expected, they found little enough to interest them on the bookshelves.

By the time they got to the manuscripts cabinets Brod was already fidgeting and looking at his watch. Casually forcing my marked promptbook on them, somewhat as a conjuror does when he makes you pick a card, I said, "I doubt if there's much here. But Sir Massey regards these holographs as the apple of his eye. The one you have there is rather defaced, I'm afraid. A lot of the others are in much better condition."

But Brod, suddenly perspiring like a pressed duckling, had a reading glass out, and Brewster was putting on a pair of micro-scope spectacles, and they were scrutinizing my little poem in the strong sunlight by the window. Brod took out notebook and pencil and made voluminous notes, occasionally nudging Brewster, who remained blank and impassive. *They* knew Bacon's hand, bless their hearts! And cryptograms were meat and drink to the likes of them.

After a while, with complete composure, Brewster said, "I don't know. It's possible the society might be interested in two or three of these manuscripts."

But I said, "I'm awfully sorry; two or three won't do, I'm afraid. Sir Massey regards this collection as a whole. He'd never break it up. There are interesting fragments by Nathaniel Field, for example, and Middleton, and Fletcher. I'm no expert, doctor, only a friendly agent."

"Sir Massey Joyce vould not refuse permission to photograph or copy certain excerpts," said Brod.

I answered, "I'm afraid he would."

Then Brewster asked, "Has this collection ever been offered for sale before?" I told him, "Never. It has never even been properly catalogued, I'm afraid."

Brewster tossed the *Hamlet* nonchalantly, as if it were a mail-order catalogue, on to a baize-covered table—I wouldn't advise a novice to play poker with that one—and he asked, "How much is Massey Joyce asking for the collection?"

Apologizing, as for an embarrassing but harmless eccentric, I said, "Well, you see, Sir Massey values things strictly in proportion to how much he personally likes them. So he swears he won't sell the manuscripts for a penny less than twenty-five thousand pounds." I laughed here, and so did Doctor Brewster, while Brod muttered something about "vine drunkards" and "devourers of the charred carcasses of slaughtered beasts."

I put the *Hamlet* back in its drawer and continued, "I know it's absurd; but when a man of Sir Massey's age has an *idée fixe*—you know? I'm afraid I've wasted your time. Well, I suppose you can't find something in your line every time you look. Oh, by the way, do you happen to know a collector named Lilienbach? He's coming next Monday. I wondered if he was all right."

I knew, of course, that Doctor Lilienbach of Philadelphia was one of the richest collectors of rare books and manuscripts in the world; and, of course, these fellows were sure to know this too.

"Lilienbach," Brod began, but Brewster cut in, "Lilienbach, Lilienbach? No, I can't say I know him. Let's not be hasty. These things take time. Look here; say I pay Sir Massey Joyce a small sum down for an option to purchase on terms to be mutually agreed?"

I said, "I shouldn't, if I were you—not until Sir Massey has had a chance to talk to Doctor Lilienbach."

Then there was a silence until, at last, Brewster said, "I'll have to call Chicago. Even *if* I were interested, I couldn't make any sort of bid before tonight."

I said, "Why not do that? Only I'm afraid you'll have to call from Ashford, Sir Massey does not believe in telephones. He thinks they cause rheumatism."

And, to cut a long story short: after a day of negotiation the Society for the Clarification of History authorized Brewster to purchase Sir Massey Joyce's Elizabethan manuscripts, with all rights pertaining thereto, for 17,599 pounds. So my old friend kept his books and had some money to support himself and the Hubbards in their declining years.

Karmesin paused. I asked, "And you got nothing?"

Karmesin said, "Massey Joyce wanted me to take half. I couldn't possibly, of course. Am I a petty larcenist to work for chicken feed? No. My amusements are few; I had my fun. For a small outlay, I had the double-barrelled pleasure of helping a friend in need at the expense of an organization which I despise."

There being a wedge of cheese left, Karmesin wrapped it in a paper napkin and put it in his pocket.

I said, "I've read nothing of your 'Baconian' document as yet."

"You will. They are preparing a book about it, and my ink is brewing for a counterblast that will shake the world. You just wait and see!"

"So there the matter ended?"

Karmesin grunted, "After dinner that night, Massey Joyce said to me, 'It is astounding that such societies can exist. They really believe Bacon wrote Shakespeare! No, really, there *are* limits! Was ever a more pernicious fable hatched by cranks?'

" 'Never,' I said.

" 'It is wonderful what people can be gulled into believing—Bacon, indeed! Why, every shopgirl knows that the plays of William Shakespeare, so-called, were written by Christopher Marlowe!' said Massey Joyce."

A LUCKY DAY FOR THE BOAR

"WELL, what the devil then, where's your title?" said Mr. Bozman, the proprietor of *The Baltimore General Press*. "I see a quotation: *Ignoscito saepe alteri numquam tibi*—which, construed, reads 'Forgive others often, but never forgive yourself.' Well?"

His editor, a timid man, murmured, "I advanced the gentleman five dollars."

"Gentleman? What the devil kind of alpaca-and-steel-mixture hack do you call gentleman? And what do you mean by five dollars? How dared you do it, sir? Silver is dug out of the ground; it does not grow on bushes. Eh? Eh?"

"We might entitle it *A Lucky Day for the Boar*, sir."

"And what does the confounded author call himself?"

"Ethan Arthur Poland. Confidentially, I think he's the man who wrote *The Raven*. Edgar Poe, no less."

"You make free with my dollars, sir. Read it over to me, mister, if you will."

"By your leave," said the editor, and read:

Self-sufficient, Colonel Hyrax came and went like a cat in the duke's palace. Nobody could deny that there was, in fact, much of the feline in his fastidiousness and in his almost inhuman composure. As chief of the secret police, Colonel Hyrax was not bound by the rules of protocol. Dread followed him, and awe—awe of the unknown—and it was whispered that the duke himself feared Colonel Hyrax.

Certainly, no one but he would have dared to detain the duke when that potentate was booted and spurred for the hunt. Yet, although he was smiling with pleasurable anticipation as he listened to the baying of his boarhounds in the courtyard below, the duke put aside his boar-spear when Colonel Hyrax appeared, and, bidding him close the door, asked, "What now, Hyrax?"

"Your Grace, I have good news."

"My foresters have beaten out a black boar of thirty stone, a monster. So be brief. Good news of what?"

"Of the conspiracy, your Grace," said Colonel Hyrax.

"I suppose," said the duke, with a harsh laugh, "I suppose you are going to tell me that my traitorous scoundrel of a nephew has named his partners in this plot against me?"

"Precisely that, your Grace," said Colonel Hyrax, with a thin smile.

"No!"

"By your Grace's leave—yes," cried Colonel Hyrax. But he looked in vain for some demonstration of relief or joy. The duke frowned.

"It is hard," he said, "it is very hard for me to believe. Are you sure, now? My nephew Stanislaus has named his friends?"

"Your Grace, I have a list of their names. They are under close arrest."

"D——it! Stanislaus is of my blood. He had—I thought he had—something of my character. Red-hot pincers could not drag a betrayal of my friends out of *me*. Milksop!"

"Yet he conspired against the life of your Grace," said Colonel Hyrax.

"I know, I know; but that was all in the family. I trapped him and he didn't lie about it. Naturally, he refused to name his collaborators. I'd have done the same in his place. Oh yes, Hyrax—touching the matter of red-hot pincers—you never dared . . . ?"

"I know my duty, your Grace," said Colonel Hyrax. "I am well aware that your blood is inviolable, and that it is death to spill one drop of it; or to offer violence, however slight, to any member of your family; or even to threaten it. Neither may any of your Grace's blood be manacled. Oh, believe me, not only was his Excellency your nephew treated with the utmost gentleness—I saw to it, when he was placed in solitary confinement by your Grace's written order, that he could not even do violence to his own person."

"And still he betrayed his comrades? He's no blood of mine!"

The duke then uttered foul accusations against his dead brother's wife. Growing calmer, he said, "More, Hyrax; tell me more." The horns sounded clear in the courtyard, but the duke threw open a casement and roared, "Let the boar wait!"

"Your Grace sentenced your nephew to perpetual solitary confinement. His Excellency was to be left to cool his head, to quote your own words."

"Did you starve him, Hyrax? You had no right to starve the boy."

"No, your Grace. He had everything of the best. The passage of time did our work for us," said Colonel Hyrax.

"Time? What time? The young fool hasn't been locked up four months. What are you talking about?"

"If I may explain?" begged Colonel Hyrax; and, his master nodding, he continued: "I had prepared for his Excellency a commodious chamber, padded at walls, floor, and ceiling with heavy quiltings of lambswool covered with gray velvet. There was a double window, out of which his Excellency might look at the wild countryside surrounding the fortress."

"Better than he deserved."

"His viands were, as I have said, of the best. But his meat was cut for him, and all his cutlery consisted in a horn spoon. For he was so violent, at first, that I feared the young gentleman might do himself a mischief."

"Ay, ay, he always was an overbred, nervous young fool. Well?"

"Then we asked his Excellency for permission to shave his head," said Colonel Hyrax. "He gave it."

"What the devil for?"

"Your Grace will see, presently. So, by his leave, we shaved off all his hair. We provided him with some quills, ink, and paper, but nothing edged or pointed. To calm him, a mild and harmless opiate was mixed with his Excellency's breakfast. He ate, and then, leaning on the casement, gazed moodily at the landscape under the morning sun. He dozed, leaning thus, for perhaps five minutes. When he opened his eyes he was looking upon a night scene with a rising moon, and the attendants were bringing his supper.

His Excellency was bewildered. 'Am I bewitched?' he asked. But since, by your Grace's order, he was *incommunicado*, the attendants were silent."

"Bewildered?" cried the duke, "So am I. From breakfast to supper—morning to moonrise—is a matter of hours. What was the purpose in bringing Stanislaus his supper five minutes after breakfast-time?"

"Pray let me explain, your Grace. The prospect beyond his window was *not* open country. It was a blank wall, upon which I had caused to be projected through a lens, by means of a powerful reflector, highly realistic scenes painted upon glass by one of the finest landscape artists in Europe. Thus, I could create a perfect illusion of the various stages of the day, and of the four seasons."

"But what for?"

"In order, your Grace, without violating your law, to let his Excellency confuse himself in his conception of *time*. Soon, he fell into a deep sleep, and an adroit barber shaved him and trimmed his nails. Men incarcerated can gauge time, to a certain extent, by the rate of growth of their beards, you see. It was necessary to *bewilder*; it was necessary to let his Excellency *force himself* to have recourse to reason, and to make his reasoning invalid. Do I make myself clear?"

"Go on."

"Hence, he would awaken—let us say—at midnight, look out of the window, see high noon; doze again, rise again in ten minutes, and—lo! and behold!—dawn. Or, awakening at dawn, he would see nothing but the rim of the setting sun, while the attendants came in with supper. Sleeping soon after, by the judicious administration of opiates, he would start up to observe another sunset. So, after a week, he asked how many months he had been there. There was no reply, of course."

"Clever, clever," said the duke.

Colonel Hyrax bowed, and continued, "Although the month was July, his Excellency awoke one morning to a scene of naked trees under a blanket of snow. Sometimes breakfast, dinner and supper would arrive at intervals of only a few minutes after the clearing of the table. Or sometimes hours might elapse, what time his Excellency, starting out of a fitful sleep, might notice that it was early autumn now, where it had been mid-winter when he last looked out.

"I took good care—since men in prison sometimes grow preternaturally observant—to age the guards and waiters, and to see to it that their uniforms showed increasing signs of wear. The chief warder was always accompanied by a pair of great dogs. At first, it was a couple of wolfhounds. I replaced these with older and older wolfhounds. Then there was a new young warder, and he had a pair of mastiffs—which, in their turn, I made appear to grow old, by a system of substitution.

"Naturally, I never entered the young gentleman's chamber myself. But I had my reports to rely upon. Your Grace—within a few weeks, your nephew believed that he had been incarcerated for an incomputable number of years! Your Grace has had the nightmare, no doubt?"

The duke said, "I have, and it's horrible. A second is an eternity, or worse. I think I understand you now, Hyrax. Go on."

"By means of concealed lamps, there was always a diffused light in the chamber which, by the judicious use of hot-air pipes was maintained at a constant temperature of precisely seventy-four degrees Fahrenheit. As his Excellency slept, his clothes were taken away and replaced by others, precisely the same in pattern, but just a little more worn. I also arranged that his clothes should be made progressively a hairsbreadth larger, so that the young gentleman grew gradually convinced that he was becoming shriveled and wasted with long imprisonment."

"Oh, clever, clever!" cried the duke, with a slight shudder. "I think that, on the whole, given the choice, I'd choose the iron boot, the thumbscrew, or the rack. Proceed."

"Ah, but there is no question of *choice*, your Grace; for this method of mine depends for its effectiveness upon complete ignorance of the surrounding circumstances. Do I make myself clear?"

"Your object being, to plant a firm illusion that there has been a prolonged passage of time, when, as a matter of fact, only hours have elapsed," said the duke.

"Just so," said Hyrax. "I have written a carefully annotated 'procedure' for your Grace's perusal. I can make four minutes last forty-eight hours, in the consciousness of the prisoner. I hasten to reassure your Grace that no common hand was laid on his Excellency, your nephew Stanislaus. His table was almost as well furnished as your Grace's own; only he had the delicacies of the season *out* of season. And, allowing for certain inevitable margins of error, the young gentleman seemed to live a long month in half an hour. Between your Grace's breakfast and dinner, he passed approximately a whole year."

"Well," said the duke, "that may teach the pup a lesson, not to plot against his poor old uncle, who used to think the world of him. Well, come to the point. What made Stanislaus betray his friends? They are my enemies, it is true, but . . . well, I think the worse of him notwithstanding."

Colonel Hyrax said, "But his Excellency did not betray his friends, your Grace."

"Will you tell me what the devil you are talking about?" roared the duke.

"I mean, he did not betray them wittingly."

"Oh? If you have deranged the rascal with your dirty drugs—" began the duke.

"No, no, your Grace. The drugs were used discreetly, and sparingly, and then only for the first three weeks. Time, time, time was the illusion with which I took the liberty of bedazzling the young gentleman—time as man knows it, through the contemplation of mere external change. Men and fashions seemed to come and go. Once, on my order, a guard let fall a newspaper. It was post-dated fifteen years: I had had one copy only printed before the type was broken up, and it was full of news of people and affairs his Excellency had never heard of."

"Most damnably clever!" exclaimed the duke. "And my poor—I mean that wretched fellow who is supposed to be my brother's son, and couldn't even keep faith with his fellow-criminals: did he write nothing?"

"Only some verses, your Grace."

"About me?"

"About worms. But I see that your Grace is anxious to be after the boar, so I will conclude for now. After the young gentleman had been in that chamber about forty days, the door was opened by a young officer in a strange uniform—gray faced with yellow—and an older officer, in the same colors, but having a dolman trimmed with sable, came in, fell on his knees, and hailed your nephew as martyr, savior, and leader. The duke, he said, was dead, the new party was in power, and Stanislaus was to sit on your throne."

The duke laughed. "Ha! And I suppose my nephew jumped for joy?"

"Not so, your Grace. He said—and I quote, so you will forgive me—he said, 'The old ruffian was kind to me once upon a time.' Then he said, 'And all my friends, I suppose, are dead, or old— which is worse.' "

"Aha!" cried the duke, "we are coming to it, now!"

"Yes, your Grace. The commanding officer said, 'If you will tell me whom you mean, your Excellency, I shall immediately ascertain.' " Whereupon, your nephew recited a list of forty names, which are on the paper which I have the honor to place in your Grace's hand."

"Hyrax," said the duke, "you are *hellishly* clever! And my nephew—how is he?"

"I was listening to the proceedings at a concealed aperture, and did not see his Excellency at first. Then, when he came into my range of vision, I was astounded. For where, a few weeks before, I had seen a sanguine young man of twenty-four, I now beheld a decrepit and enfeebled man of sixty!"

The duke was silent. Colonel Hyrax pointed to the paper upon which the names of the conspirators were written. "Your Grace will hang them?" he asked.

"No. I shall shock the wits out of them by pardoning them, and make forty friends into the bargain. Where's Stanislaus?"

"Asleep, your Grace," said Colonel Hyrax.

"You are an astonishingly clever man, Hyrax," said the duke. "Did I not say that if you cleared this matter up I'd make a nobleman of you?"

"The work is its own reward, your Grace," said Hyrax.

"No, you have earned my gratitude. I hereby confer upon you the Barony of Opa, with all lands, rents, and revenues pertaining thereunto."

"Oh, your Grace! Words cannot express—"

"—Save them, then. Leave me, now."

Hyrax having bowed himself out of his presence, the duke called for his secretary. A soberly attired gentleman came in and made his obeisance. "Your Grace?"

"Colonel Hyrax is now Colonel, the Baron Opa. Make a note of it."

"Yes, your Grace."

The duke paced the floor, tugging at his beard. "And write me an order to the Lord Provost," he said. "Write as follows:— 'Bearing in mind the new dignity of Colonel Hyrax, whom we have recently created Baron of Opa, you will procure a silk cord and hang him forthwith'." Scrawling his signature at the foot of this document, and impressing the warm wax with his great carnelian ring, the duke muttered, "One could no longer sleep with such a man awake. He is too clever by half."

A nameless cold had crept into his heart. He looked long and anxiously at the morning sun, and listened with more than usual attention to the portentous ticking of the great bronze clock. Presently, he said to his secretary, "Dismiss the men. I hunt no boar today."

"Yes, your Grace."

"I desire to see Stanislaus."

"Shall he be sent for?"

"No. I go to him."

The secretary, a good-hearted man, ventured to ask, "Oh please, your Grace—is it your gracious intention magnanimously to pardon the unhappy young gentleman?"

The duke growled, "No. My Grace's intention is humbly to beg the unlucky young gentleman, out of his magnanimity, *to pardon me.*"

The proprietor said, "You gave this person five dollars, you say?"

"He asked twenty," said the editor. "I advanced him five."

"You throw my dollars about like rice at a wedding, my friend. Yes, you have my leave to print. Let the fellow have five dollars more, if he presses. A Latin title is a drug, sir, a drug. Take a title out of context," said Mr. Bozman. "Out of context, out of context. And since I am paying for the job and writing it too, sign it Bozman—John Helliwell Bozman. Incidentally, you owe me five dollars."

So saying, the proprietor of *The Baltimore General Press* walked sedately out of doors.

VOICES IN THE DUST OF ANNAN

I LANDED ON THE northeast coast, with tinned goods and other trade goods such as steel knives, beads, and sweet chocolate, intending to make my way to the ruins of Annan.

A chieftain of the savages of the Central Belt warned me not to go to The Bad Place. That was his name for the ancient ruins of the forgotten city of Annan, a hundred miles to the southeast. Some of the tribesmen called it The Dead Place, or The Dark Place. He called it The Bad Place. He was a grim, but honorable old ruffian, squat and hairy and covered with scars. Over a pot of evil-smelling black beer—they brew it twice a year, with solemn ceremony, and everyone gets hideously drunk—he grew communicative, and, as the liquor took hold of him, boastful. He showed me his tattooing: every mark meant something, so that his history was pricked out on his skin. When a chieftain of the Central Belt dies he is flayed, and his hide is hung up in the hut that is reserved for holy objects: so he lives in human memory. Showing his broken teeth in a snarling smile, he pointed to a skillfully executed fish on his left arm: it proved that he had won a great victory over the Fish-Eaters of the north. A wild pig on his chest celebrated the massacre of the Pig Men of the northwest. He hiccuped a bloody story, caressing a black-and-red dog that lay at his feet and watched me with murderous yellow eyes. . . . Oh, the distances he had travelled, the men he had killed, the women he had ravished, the riches he had plundered! He knew everything. He liked me—had I not given him a fine steel knife? So he would give me some good advice.

"I could keep you here if I liked," he said, "but you are my friend, and if you want to go you may go. I will even send ten armed men with you. You may need them. If you are traveling southwards you must pass through the country of the Red Men. They eat men when they can catch them, and move fast: they come and go. Have no fear, however, of the Bird Men. For a handful of beads and a little wire—especially wire—they will do anything. My men will not go with you to The Bad Place. Nobody ever goes to The Bad Place. Even I would not go to The Bad Place, and I am the bravest man in the world. Why must you go? Stay. Live under my protection. I will give you a wife. Look. You can have her—" He jerked a spatulate thumb in the direction of a big, swarthy girl with greased hair who squatted, almost naked, a couple of yards away. "—She is one of mine. But you can have her. No man has touched her yet. Marry her. Stay."

I said: "Tell me, why have you—even you, Chief—stayed away from that place?"

He grew grave. "I fear no man and no beast," he said.

"But—?"

"But." He gulped some more black beer. "There are things."

"What things?"

"Things. Little people." He meant fairies. "I'll fight anything I can see. But what of that which man cannot see? Who fights that? Stay away from The Bad Place. Marry *her* . . . Stay here. Feel her—fat! Don't go. Nobody goes. . . . Hup! I like you. You are my friend. You must stay here."

I gave him a can of peaches. He crowed like a baby. "You are my friend," he said, "and if you want to go, then go. But if you get away, come back."

"*If?*" I said.

"If."

"I don't believe in fairies," I said.

His eyebrows knotted, his fists knotted, and he bared his teeth. "Are you saying that what I say is not true?" he shouted.

"King, Great Chief," I said, "I believe, I believe. What you say is true."

"If I had not given my word I should have had you killed for that," he grunted. "But I have gi-given my word. . . . Hup! My-my word is a word. I . . . you . . . go, go!"

Next morning he was ill. I gave him magnesia in a pot of water, for which he expressed gratitude. That day I set out with ten squat, sullen warriors; killers, men without fear.

But when we came in sight of the place that was called The Bad Place, The Dark Place, or The Dead Place, they stopped. For no consideration would they walk another step forward. I offered each man a steel knife. Their terror was stronger than their desire. "Not even for that," said their leader.

I went on alone.

It was a dead place because there was no life in it; and therefore it was also a dark place. No grass grew there. It had come to nothingness. Not even the coarse, hardy weeds that find a root-hold in the uncooled ashes of burnt-out buildings pushed their leaves out of its desolation. Under the seasonal rain it must have been a quagmire. Now, baked by the August sun, it was a sort of ash-heap, studded with gray excrescences that resembled enormous cinders. A dreary, dark gray, powdery valley went down; a melancholy dust-heap of a hill crept up and away. As I looked I saw something writhe and come up out of the hillside—it came down toward me with a sickening, wriggling run, and it was pale gray like a ghost. I drew my pistol. Then the gray thing pirouetted and danced. It was nothing but dust, picked up by a current of warm air. The cold hand that had got hold of my heart relaxed, and my heart fell back into my stomach, where it had already sunk.

I went down. This place was so dead that I was grateful for the company of the flies that had followed me. The sun struck like a floodlight out of a clean blue sky; every crumb of grit threw a clear-cut black shadow in the dust. A bird passed, down and up, quick as the flick of a whip, on the trail of a desperate dragonfly. Yet here, in a white-hot summer afternoon, I felt that I was going down, step by step, into the black night of the soul. This was a bad place.

The dust clung to me. I moved slowly, between half-buried slabs of shattered granite. Evening was coming. A breeze that felt like a hot breath on my neck stirred the ruins of the ancient city; dust devils twisted and flirted and fell; the sun gray-red. At last I found something that had been a wall, and pitched my tent close to it. Somehow it was good to have a wall behind me. There was nothing to be afraid of—there was absolutely nothing. Yet I was afraid. What is it that makes a comfortable man go out with a pickaxe to poke among the ruins of ancient cities? I was sick with nameless terror. But fear breeds pride. I could not go back. And I was tired, desperately tired. If I did not sleep I would break.

I ate and lay down. Sleep was picking me away, leaf by leaf. Bad place . . . dead place . . . dark place . . . little people. . . .

Before I fell asleep I thought I heard somebody singing a queer, wailing song:—*Oh-oooo, oh-oooo, oh-oooo!* It rose and descended—it conveyed terror. It might have been an owl, or some other night-bird; or it might have been the wind in the ruins; or a half-dream. It sounded almost human, though. I started awake, clutching my pistol. I could have sworn that the wail was forming words. What words? They sounded like some debased sort of Arabic:—

Ookil' karabin
Ookil' karabin
Isapara mibanara
Ikil' karabin
Ookil' karabin

As I sat up the noise stopped. Yes, I thought, I was dreaming; I lay back and went to sleep. Centuries of silence lay in the dust.

All the same, in that abominable loneliness I felt that I was not alone. I awoke five times before dawn, to listen. There was nothing. Even the flies had gone away. Yet when day broke I observed that something strange had happened.

My socks had disappeared.

In the dust, that powdery dust in which the petal of a flower would have left its imprint, there were no tracks. Yet the flap of my tent was unfastened, and my socks were gone.

For the next three days I sifted the detritus of that dead city, fumbling and feeling after crumbs of evidence, and listening to the silence. My pickaxe pecked out nothing but chips of stone and strange echoes. On the second day I unearthed some fragments of crumbling glass and shards of white, glazed pottery, together with a handful of narrow pieces of iron which fell to nothing as I touched them. I also found a small dish of patterned porcelain, inscribed with five letters—R E S E N—part of some inscription. It was sad and strange that this poor thing should have survived the smashing of the huge edifices and noble monuments of that great city. But all the time, I felt that someone, or something, was watching me an inch beyond my field of vision. On the third day I found a red drinking-vessel, intact, and a cooking-pot of some light, white metal, with marks of burning on the bottom of it and some charred powder inside. The housewife to whom this pot belonged was cooking some sort of stew, no doubt, when the wrath of God struck the city.

When the blow fell, that city must have ceased to be in less time than it takes to clap your hands: it fell like the cities of the plain when the fire came down from heaven. Here, as in the ruins of Pompeii, one might discover curiously pathetic ashes and highly individual dust. I found the calcined skeleton of a woman, clutching, in the charred vestiges of loving arms, the skeletal outline of a newly-born child. As I touched these remains they broke like burnt paper. Not far away, half-buried in a sort of volcanic cinder, four twisted lumps of animal charcoal lay in the form of a cross, the center of which was a shapeless mass of glass: this had been a sociable drinking-party. This lump of glass melted and ran into a blob, the outlines of which suggest the map of Africa. But in the equatorial part of it so to speak one could distinguish the base of a bottle. I also found a tiny square of thin, woven stuff. It must have been a handkerchief, a woman's handkerchief. Some whimsy of chance let it stay intact. In one corner of it was embroidered a Roman letter A. Who was A? I seem to see some fussy, fastidious gentlewoman, discreetly perfumed—a benevolent tyrant at home, but every inch a lady. Deploring the decadence of the age, she dabbed this delicate twenty-five square inches of gauzy nothingness at one sensitive nostril. Then—psst! She and the house in which she lived were swept away in one lick of frightful heat. And the handkerchief fluttered down on her ashes.

Nearby, untouched by time and disaster, stood a low wall of clay bricks. On this wall was an inscription in chalk. A child must have scrawled it. It said: *Lidia is a dirty pig.* Below it lay the unidentifiable remains of three human beings. As I looked, the air-currents stirred the dust. Swaying and undulating like a ballet dancer, a fine gray powdery corkscrew spun up and threw itself at my feet.

That night, again, I thought I heard singing. But what was there to sing? Birds? There were no birds. Nevertheless, I lay awake. I was uneasy. There was no moon. I saw that my watch said 12:45. After that I must have slipped into the shallow end of sleep, because I opened my eyes—instinct warned me to keep still—and saw that more than two hours had passed. I felt rather than heard a little furtive sound. I lay quiet and listened. Fear and watchfulness had sharpened my ears. In spite of the beating of my heart I heard a *tink-tink* of metal against metal. My flashlight was under my left hand; my pistol was in my right. I breathed deeply. The metal clinked again. Now I knew where to look. I aimed the flashlight at the noise, switched on a broad beam of bright light, and leapt up with a roar of that mad rage that comes out of fear. Something was caught in the light. The light paralyzed it: the thing was glued in the shining, white puddle—it had enormous eyes. I fired at it—I mean, I aimed at it and pressed my trigger, but had forgotten to lift my safety-catch. Holding the thing in the flashlight beam, I struck at it with the barrel of the pistol. I was cruel because I was afraid. It squealed, and something cracked. Then I had it by the neck. If it was not a rat it smelled like a rat. *Oh-oooo, oh-oooo, oh-oooo!* it wailed, and I heard something scuffle outside. Another voice wailed *oh-oooo, oh-oooo, oh-oooo!* A third voice picked it up. In five seconds, the hot, dark night was full of a most woebegone crying. Five seconds later there was silence, except for the gasping of the cold little creature under my hand.

I was calm now, and I saw that it was not a rat. It was something like a man; a little, distorted man. The light hurt it, yet it could not look away—the big eyes contracted, twitching and flickering, out of a narrow and repulsive face fringed with a pale hair.

"*O, O, O,*" it said—the wet, chisel-toothed mouth was quivering on the edge of a word.

I noticed then that it was standing on something gray—looked again, and saw my woolen jacket. It had been trying to take this jacket away. But in the right-hand pocket there were a coin and a small key: they had struck together and awakened me.

I was no longer afraid so I became kind. "Calm," I said, as one talks to a dog, "Calm, calm, calm! Quiet now, quiet!"

The little white one held up a wrist from which drooped a skinny, naked hand like a mole's paw, and whispered:

"*Oh-oooo.*"

"Sit!" I said.

It was terrified and in pain. I had broken its wrist: I should say *his* wrist—he was a sort of man; a male creature; wretched, filthy and dank, dwarfish, debased; greenish-white like mildew, smelling like mildew, cold and wetly-yielding like mildew; rat-toothed, rat-eared and chinless; yet not unlike a man. If he had stood upright he would have been about three feet tall.

This, then, was the nameless thing that had struck such terror into the bloody old chieftain of the savages of the Central Belt— this bloodless, chinless thing without a forehead, whose limbs were like the tendrils of a creeping plant that sprouts in the dark, and who cringed, twittering and whimpering, at my feet. Its eyes were large like a lemur's. The ears were long, pointed, and almost transparent; they shone sickly-pink in the light, and I could see that they were reticulated with thin, dark veins. There had been some attempt at clothing—a kind of primitive jacket and leggings of some thin gray fur, tattered and indescribably filthy. My stomach turned at the feel of it, and its deathly, musty smell.

This, then, was one of the fairies, one of the little people of The Dead Place, and I had it by the neck.

I may say, at this point, that I have always believed in fairies. By "fairies" I do not mean little, delicate, magical, pretty creatures with butterfly wings, living among the flowers and drinking nectar out of bluebell blossoms. I do not believe in such fairies. But I do believe in the little people—the gnomes, elves, pucks, brownies, pixies, and leprechauns of legend. Belief in these little people is as old as the world, universal, and persistent. In the stories, you remember, the outward appearance of the little people is fairly constant. They are dwarfish. They have big eyes and long, pointed features. They come out at night, and have the power to make themselves invisible. Sometimes they are mischievous. They have been known to steal babies from their cradles. The horrified mother, starting awake, finds, in the place of her plump, rosy infant, a shriveled little horror. The little people have carried her baby away and left one of their own in its place—a changeling as it is called. It is best to keep on the good side of the little people, because they can play all kinds of malevolent tricks—spoil the butter, frighten the cows, destroy small objects. You will have observed that they have no power to seriously injure mankind; yet they carry with them the terror of the night. In some parts of the world, peasants placate the little people by leaving out a bowl of hot porridge or milk for them to drink, for they are always hungry and always cold. Note that. Every child has read the story of the cold lad of the hill: A poor cobbler, having spent his last few coins on a piece of leather, fell asleep, too tired to work. When he awoke in the morning he found that the leather had been worked with consummate skill into a beautiful pair of slippers. He sold these slippers and bought a larger piece of leather, which he left on the bench together with a bowl of hot soup. Then he pretended to fall asleep and saw, out of the corner of his eye, a tiny, pale, shivering, naked man who crept in and set to work with dazzling speed. Next morning there were two pairs of slippers. This went on for several days. Prosperity returned to the house of the cobbler. His wife, to reward the little man, knitted him a little cloak with a hood. They put the garment on the bench. That night the little man came again. He saw the cloak and hood, put them on, with a squeal of joy, capered up and down the cobbler's bench admiring himself, and at last sprang out of the window saying, "I have taken your cloak, I have taken your hood, and the cold lad of the hill will do no more good." He never appeared again. He had got what he wanted: a woolen cloak with a hood.

The little people hate the cold, it appears.

Now if they are sensitive to cold and hunger, as all the stories indicate, they must be people of flesh and blood. Why not? There are all kinds of people. There is no reason why, in the remote past, certain people should not have gone to live underground, out of the reach of fierce and powerful enemies. For example, there used to be a race of little men in north Britain called the Picts. History records them as fierce and cunning little border raiders—men of the heather, who harried the Roman garrisons in ancient times and stole whatever they could lay their hands on. These Picts— like the African bushmen who, by the way, were also very little people—could move so quickly and surely that they seemed to have a miraculous gift of invisibility. In broad daylight a Pict could disappear, and not a single heather-blossom quivered over his hiding place. The Picts disappeared off the face of the earth at last. Yet, for centuries, in certain parts of Scotland, the farmers and shepherds continued to fear them. They were supposed to have gone underground, into the caves, from whence they sometimes emerged to carry off a sheep, a woman, a cooking-pot or a child.

Superstition turned these small, terrified creatures into fairies. In Cornwall again, many people used to believe in piskies—little creatures with big eyes, who wrapped themselves up in garments with pointed hoods and whom it was wise to placate with bowls of milk. It seems to me not unreasonable to assume that, during the long, drawn out periods of strife on the western borders of Britain, certain little weak people went underground, and made a new life for themselves secure in the darkness of the caves. Living in the dark, of course, they would grow pale. After many generations they would have developed a cat's faculty for seeing in the dark. And for feeling their way they would have developed a bushman's knack of disappearing—of keeping absolutely still in cover. But they were human beings and could not entirely divorce themselves from their fellows; so they stayed—half-yearning, and half-terrified—not far from ordinary human habitation. The little people are supposed to know the whereabouts of great buried treasures. This also is possible. Their remote ancestors may have taken their riches with them to bury, meaning to unearth them in safer times which never came. Again, these strange underground men, who knew every stone, every tree, and every tuft of grass in their country, may easily have come across treasures buried by other men. They would have retained the human instinct to pick up and carry away something bright or valuable, and so they carried everything that they found to the mysterious places below the surface of the earth where they lived their mysterious lives; and since they had no real use for the money they had acquired, they let it accumulate. In how many fairy tales has one read of the well-disposed little one who left behind him a bright gold coin.

I am convinced that ever since frightened men began to run away and hide, there have been little people, in other words, fairies. And such was the drooling, nightmarish little thing that trembled in my grip that night in the tent.

I remembered, then, how frightened I had been. As I thought of all the awe that such creatures had inspired through the ages, I began to laugh. The little man—I had better call him a man—listened to me. He stopped whimpering. His ears quivered, then he gave out a queer, breathless, hiccuping sound, faint as the ticking of a clock. "Are you human?" I asked.

He trembled, and laboriously made two noises: *"Oon-ern."*

He was trying to repeat what I had said. I led him to an angle of the tent so that he could not escape, and tied up his wrist with an elastic plaster. He looked at it, gibbering. Then I gave him a piece of highly-sweetened chocolate. He was afraid of that too. I bit off a corner and chewed it, saying, "Good. Eat."

I was absurdly confident that, somehow, he would understand me. He tried to say what I had said—*Oo-ee*, and crammed the chocolate into his mouth. For half a second he slobbered, twitching with delight, then the chocolate was gone. I patted his head. The touch of it made me shudder, yet I forced my hand to a caress. I was the first man on earth who had ever captured a fairy: I would have taken him to my bosom. I smiled at him. He blinked at me. I could see by the movement of his famished little chest that he was a little less afraid of me. I found another piece of chocolate and offered it to him. But in doing so, I lowered my flashlight. The chocolate was flicked out of my hand. I was aware of something that bobbed away and ran between my legs. Before I could turn, the little man was gone. The flap of the tent was moving. If it had not been for that, and a stale, dirty smell, I might have thought I had been dreaming.

I turned the beam of my flashlight to the ground.

This time, the little man had left tracks.

As I was to discover, the little people of The Dead Place used to cover their tracks by running backwards on all fours and blowing dust over the marks their hands and feet had made. But my little man had not had time to do this tonight.

Dawn was beginning to break. I filled my pockets with food and set out. Nothing was too light to leave a mark in that place, but the same quality that made the fine dust receptive made every mark impermanent. I began to run. The little man's tracks resembled those of a gigantic mole. The red dust sun was up and the heat of the day was coming down, when I came to the end of his trail. He had scuttled under a great, gray heap of shattered stone. This had been a vast—possibly a noble—building. Now it was a rubbish heap; packed tight by the inexorable pull of the earth through the centuries. Here was fairyland, somewhere in the depths of the earth.

Enormous edifices had been crushed and scattered like burnt biscuits thrown to the wild birds. The crumbs were identifiable. The shape of the whole was utterly lost. The loneliness was awful. Inch by inch I felt myself slipping into that spiritual twilight which sucks down to the black night of the soul. The tracks of the little man had disappeared—the dust was always drifting, and the contours of the lost city were perpetually changing. Yesterday was a memory. Tomorrow was a dream. Then tomorrow became yesterday— a memory; and memory blurred and twirled away with the dust devils. I was sick. There was a bad air in the ruins of Annan. I might have died, or run away, if there had not been the thunderstorm.

It threatened for forty-eight hours. I thought that I was delirious. Everything was still, dreadfully still. The air was thick, and hard to breathe. It seemed to me that from some indefinable part of the near distance I heard again that thin, agonized singing which I had heard once before. Male and female voices wailed a sort of hymn:—

> *Aaah, Balasamo,*
> *Balasamo! Oh!*
> *Sarna Corpano! . . . Oh-Oh!*
> *Binno Mosha*
> *Sada Rosha*
> *Chu mila Balasamo! . . . Oh!*

Then the storm broke, and I thanked God for it. It cleared the air and it cleared my head. The sky seemed to shake and reverberate like a sheet of iron. Lightning feinted and struck, and the rain fell. Between the thunder I could still hear the singing. As dawn came the storm rumbled away, and the aspect of the ruins was changed.

Annan wore a ragged veil of mist. Thin mud was running away between the broken stones. The sun was coming up and in a little while the dust would return; but for the moment the rain had washed the face of the ruin.

So I found the lid of the underworld.

It was a disc of eroded metal that fitted a hole in the ground. I struck it with my hammer: it fell to pieces. The pieces dropped away, and out of the hole in the ground there rose a dusty, sickening, yet familiar smell. The hole was the mouth of an ancient sewer. I could see the rusty remains of a metal ladder. The top rung was solid—I tried it with my foot. The next rung supported my weight. I went down.

The fifth rung broke, and I fell.

I remember that I saw a great white light—then a great dark. Later—I do not know how much later—I opened my eyes. I knew that I was alive, because I felt pain. But I was not lying where I had fallen. I could see no circle of daylight such as I had seen in falling, at the mouth of the manhole. There was nothing to be seen: I was in the dark. And I could hear odd little glottal voices.

"Water!" I said.

"Ah-awa," said a thin, whining voice. Something that felt like a cracked earthenware saucer was pressed against my lips. It contained a spoonful or two of cold water; half a mouthful. The cracked earthenware saucer was taken away empty and brought back full. I took hold of it, to steady it.

It was a little cupped hand, a live hand.

I knew then that I had fallen down into the underground world of the little people that haunt the desolate ruin called Annan, or The Bad Place. I was in fairyland. But my right leg was broken. My flashlight was broken, and I was in the dark.

There was nothing to be done. I could only lie still.

The little people squatted around me in a circle. One high, ecstatic, piping voice began to sing:

> *Ookil' karabin,*
> *Ookil' karabin!*

Thirty or forty voices screeched:—

> *Isapara mibanara,*
> *Ikil' karabin!*

Then, abruptly, the singing stopped. Something was coming. These little people knew the art of making fire, and understood the use of light. One of them was holding a tiny vessel, in which flickered a dim, spluttering flame no larger than a baby's fingernail. It was not what we would call illumination. It was better than darkness, it permitted one to see, at least, a shadow. You will never know the comfort that I found in that tiny flame. I wept for joy. My sobbing jolted my broken leg, and I must have fainted. I was a wounded man, remember. Shivering in a wet cold that came from me and not from the place in which I lay, I felt myself rising in waves of nausea out of a horrible emptiness.

The little people had gone, all but one. The one that stayed had my elastic plaster on his left wrist. His right hand was cupped, and it held water, which I drank. Then he made a vague gesture in the direction of my pockets—he wanted chocolate. I saw this in the light of the little lamp, which still flickered. His shadow danced; he looked like a rat waltzing with a ghost. I had some chocolate in my pocket, and gave him a little. The light was dying. I pointed at it with a forefinger and gesticulated *up, up, up* with my hands.

He ran away and came back with another lamp.

I can tell you now that the oil that feeds those little lamps is animal fat—the fat of rats. The wicks of the lamps are made of twisted rat-hair. The little men of Annan have cultivated rats, since they went underground. There are hereditary rat-herds, just as there used to be hereditary shepherds and swine-herds. I have learned something—not much—of the habits of the little men of the dust in Annan. They dress in rat-skin clothes and have scraped out runs, or burrows, which extend for miles to the thirty-two points of the compass. They have no government and no leaders. They are sickly people. They are perishing.

Yet they are men of a sort. They have fire, although they cannot tolerate the glare of honest daylight. They have—like all of their kind—a buried treasure of useless coins. They have the vestiges of a language, but they are always cold. The poor creature whose wrist I broke had wanted my woolen jacket; now I gave it to him, and he wept for joy. They cultivated fungi—which I have eaten, not without relish—augment their diet of the rank meat which they get by butchering the gray creatures that provide them with food, fat, and fur. But they are always hungry. The rats are getting slower and less reliable in their breeding: the herds are thinning out.

My little man kept me supplied with meat and water. In the end I began to understand the meaning of his whispering and snuffling underworld language. This fairy, this man of the dust of Annan, was kind to me in his way. He adored me as a fallen god. Sometimes, when I raved and wept in delirium, he ran away. But he always came back. My leg was throbbing. I knew that infection was taking hold of the wound, and began to lose hope down in the dark. I tried to detach my mind from the miserable condition of my body. I listened to the strange songs of the rat-people. It was through the chant *Balasamo* that I learned their language. It came to me in a flash of revelation as I lay listening, *Balasamo, Balasamo* . . . The tune wove in and out. It gave me no peace. I had heard something like it at home. Doctor Opel had been lecturing on ancient music. . . .

Suddenly I understood. I remembered.

> *Balasamo,*
> *Balasamo,*
> *Sarnacorpano!*

This was a song five hundred years old. It used to be a marching song during World Wars I, II and III. The words, which time had corrupted and misery debased, should have been:

> *Bless 'em all,*
> *Bless 'em all,*
> *Sergeants and Corporals and all!*
> *There'll be no promotion*
> *This side of the ocean*
> *So cheer up my lads, bless 'em all!*

Similarly, *Ookil' karabin* meant *Who Killed Cock Robin.*

And, of course, *Annan* came down, whine by whine, through *Unnon* and *Lunnon* from *London!* The little people spoke archaic English. I could see, then, something of their melancholy history. I could see the proud city dwellers going down to become shelter dwellers at the outbreak of the Atom War, The Ten Minute War of 19 . . . , 19 . . . . I forget the exact date . . . My head is swimming . . . My little rat-man watches me with terrified eyes. Somewhere his people are singing . . . But the light is dying, and so am I. . . .

WHATEVER HAPPENED TO CORPORAL CUCKOO?

S EVERAL thousand officers and privates of the U. S. Army who fought in Europe in World War II can bear witness to certain basic facts in this otherwise incredible story.

Let me refresh my witnesses' memories:

The Cunard White Star liner the *Queen Mary* sailed from Greenock, at the mouth of the river Clyde, on July 6th, 1945, bound for New York, packed tight with passengers. No one who made that voyage can have forgotten it: there were fourteen thousand men on board, a few ladies, and one dog. The dog was a gentle, intelligent German shepherd, saved from slow and painful death by a young American officer in Holland. I was told that this brave animal, exhausted, and weak with hunger, had tried to jump over a high barbed wire fence, and had got caught in the barbs on the top strand, where it hung for days, unable to go forward or backward. The young officer helped it down, and so the dog fell in love with the man, and the man fell in love with the dog. Pets are not allowed on troopships. Still, the young officer managed to get his dog on board. Rumor has it that his entire company swore that they would not return to the United States without the dog, so that the authorities were persuaded to stretch a point, just for once: this is what Kipling meant when he referred to the power of the dog. Everyone who sailed on the *Queen Mary* from Greenock on July 6, 1945 remembers that dog. It came aboard in a deplorable state, arching its bedraggled back to ease its poor injured stomach, and when you stroked it, you felt its skeleton under the sickly, staring coat. After about three days of affectionate care—half a hundred strong, hungry men begged or stole bits of meat for its sake—the dog began to recover. By July 11, when the *Queen Mary* docked in New York, the dog was taking a dog's interest in a soft rubber ball with which several officers were playing on the sun deck.

I bring all this back into memory to prove that I was there, as a war correspondent, on my way to the Pacific. Since I was wearing battledress and a beard, I, also, must have been conspicuous that voyage. And the secret school of illicit crapshooters must remember me with nostalgic affection: I arrived in New York with exactly fifteen cents, and had to borrow five dollars from an amiable Congregationalist minister named John Smith—who also will testify to the fact that I was on board. If further evidence were needed, a lady nurse, Lieutenant Grace Dimichele, of Vermont, took my photograph as we came into port.

But in the excitement of that tremendous moment, when thousands of men were struggling and jostling, laughing and crying, and snapping cameras at the New York skyline which is the most beautiful in the world, I lost Corporal Cuckoo. I have made exhaustive enquiries as to his whereabouts, but that extraordinary man had disappeared like a puff of smoke.

Surely, there must be scores of men who retain some memory of Cuckoo, whom they must have seen hundreds and hundreds of times on the *Queen Mary*, between July 6th and July 11, 1945.

He was a light-haired man of medium height, but he must have weighed at least a hundred and ninety pounds, for he was ponderously built, and had enormously heavy bones. I beg my fellow passengers to remember, if they can. He had watery eyes of greenish-gray, and limped a little on his right leg. His teeth were powerful—large, square, and slightly protruding; but generally he kept them covered with his thick, curiously wrinkled lips. People in general are unobservant, I know, but no one who saw Corporal Cuckoo could fail to remember his scars. There was a frightful indentation in his skull, between his left eyebrow and his right ear. When I first noticed him, I remembered an axe murder at which I shuddered many years ago when I was a crime reporter. "He must have an extraordinary constitution if he lives to walk around with a scar like that," I thought. His chin and throat were puckered scar tissue such as marks the place where flesh has been badly burned and well healed. Half of his right ear was missing and close by there was another scar, from cheekbone to mastoid. The back of his right hand appeared to have been hacked with a knife—I counted at least four formidable cuts, all old and white and deep. He conveyed this impression: that a long time ago, a number of people had got together to butcher him with hatchets, sabres, and knives, and that, in spite of their most determined efforts, he had survived. For all his scars were old. Yet the man was young—not more than thirty-five as I guessed.

He filled me with a burning curiosity. One of you *must* remember him! He went about, surly and unsociable, smoking cigarettes which he never took out of his mouth—he smoked them down and spat the ends out only when the fire touched his lips. That, I thought, must be why his eyes are so watery. He moped about, thinking, or brooding. He was particularly addicted to loitering on the stairs and lurking in dark corners. I made tentative enquiries about him around the decks; but just then everyone was passionately interested in an officer who looked like Spencer Tracy. But in the end I found out for myself.

Liquor, also, was prohibited on troopships. Having been warned of this, I took the precaution of smuggling some bottles of whiskey aboard. On the first day out I offered a drink to a captain of Infantry. Before I knew where I was, I had made seventeen new friends who overwhelmed me with affability and asked for my autograph; so that on the second day, having thrown the last of the empty bottles out of the porthole, I was glad to sponge a drink off Mr. Charles Bennett, the playwright, of Hollywood, California. (He, too, if his modesty permits, will bear witness that I am telling the truth.) He gave me a ginger ale bottle full of good Scotch, which I concealed in the blouse of my battledress, not daring to let any of my friends know that I had it. Late in the evening of the third day, I withdrew to a quiet spot where there was a strong enough diffusion of yellow light for me to read by. I intended to struggle again through some of the poems of François Villon, and to refresh myself at intervals with a spot of Mr. Bennett's Scotch. It was hard to find an unoccupied place beyond locked doors on the *Queen Mary* at that time, but I found one. I was trying to read Villon's *Ballade of Good Counsel*, which that great poet wrote in medieval underworld slang, which is all but incomprehensible even to erudite Frenchmen who have studied the argot of the period. I repeated the first two lines aloud, hoping to talk some new meaning into them:

Car ou soie porteur de bulles
pipeur ou hasardeur de dez

Then a languid voice said: "Hello, there! What do you know about it?"

I looked up and saw the sombre, scarred face of the mysterious Corporal half-in and half-out of the shadows. There was nothing to do but offer him a drink for I had the bottle in my hand, and he was looking at it. He thanked me curtly, half emptied the little bottle in one gulp and returned it to me. *"Pipeur ou hasardeur de dez,"* he said sighing. "That's old stuff. Do you like it, sir?"

I said: "Very much indeed. What a great man Villon must have been. Who else could have used such debased language to such effect? Who else could have taken thieves' patter—which is always ugly—and turned it into beautiful poetry?"

"You understand it, eh?" he asked, with a half laugh.

"I can't say that I do," I said, "but it certainly makes poetry."

"Yes, I know.

"Pipeur ou hasardeur de dez. You might as well try to make poetry out of something like this: 'I don't care if you run some come-to-Jesus racket, or shoot craps . . .' Who are you? What's the idea? It's a hell of a long time since they allowed you to wear a beard in the Army."

"War correspondent," I said. "My name is Kersh. You might as well finish this."

He emptied the little bottle and said: "Thanks, Mr. Kersh. My name is Cuckoo."

He threw himself down beside me, striking the deck like a sack of wet sand. "Yeahp . . . I think I will sit down," he said. Then he took my little book in his frightfully scarred right hand, flapped it against his knee, and then gave it back to me. *"Hasardeur de dez!"* he said, in an outlandish accent.

"You read Villon, I see," I said.

"No, I don't. I'm not much of a reader."

"But you speak French?"

"So what?"

"Where did you learn it?" I asked.

"In France."

"On your way home now?"

"I guess so."

"You're not sorry, I daresay."

"No, I guess not."

"You were in France?"

"Holland."

"In the army long?"

"Quite a while."

"Do you like it?"

"Sure. It's alright, I guess. Where are you from?"

"London," I said.

He said, "I've been there."

"And where do you come from?" I asked.

"What? . . . Me? . . . Oh, from New York, I guess."

"And how did you like London?" I asked.

"It's improved."

"Improved? I was afraid you'd seen it at a disadvantage, what with the bombing, and all that," I said.

"Oh, London's alright, I guess."

"You should have been there before the war, Corporal Cuckoo."

"I was there before the war."

"You must have been very young then," I said.

Corporal Cuckoo replied: "Not so damn young."

I said: "I'm a war correspondent, and newspaper man, and so I have the right to ask impertinent questions. I might, you know, write a piece about you for my paper. What sort of name is Cuckoo? I've never heard it before."

For the sake of appearances I had taken out a notebook and pencil. The corporal said: "My name isn't really Cuckoo. It's a

French name, originally—*Le Cocu*. You know what that means, don't you?"

Somewhat embarrassed, I replied: "Well, if I remember rightly, a man who is *cocu* is a man whose wife has been unfaithful to him."

"That's right."

"Have you any family?"

"No."

"But you have been married?" I asked.

"Plenty."

"What do you intend to do when you get back to the States, Corporal Cuckoo?"

He said: "Grow flowers, and keep bees and chickens."

"All alone?"

"That's right," said Corporal Cuckoo.

"Flowers, bees and chickens! . . . What kind of flowers?" I asked.

"Roses," he said, without hesitation. Then he added: "Maybe a little later on I'll go south."

"What on earth for?" I asked.

"Turpentine."

Corporal Cuckoo, I thought, must be insane. Thinking of this, it occurred to me that his brain might have been deranged by the wound that had left that awful scar on his head. I said: "They seem to have cut you a bit, Corporal Cuckoo."

"Yes, sir, a little bit here and there," he said, chuckling. "Yeahp, I've taken plenty in my time."

"So I should think, Corporal. The first time I saw you I was under the impression that you'd got caught up in some machinery, or something of the sort."

"What do you mean, machinery?"

"Oh, no offense, Corporal, but those wounds on your head and face and neck haven't the appearance of wounds such as you might get from any weapon of modern warfare—"

"Who said they were?" said Corporal Cuckoo, roughly. Then he filled his lungs with air, and blew out a great breath which ended in an exclamation: "*Phoo*—wow! What was that stuff you gave me to drink?"

"Good Scotch. Why?"

"It's good alright. I didn't ought to drink it. I've laid off the hard stuff for God knows how many years. It goes to my head. I didn't ought to touch it."

"Nobody asked you to empty a twelve-ounce ginger ale bottle full of Scotch in two drinks," I said resentfully.

"I'm sorry, mister. When we get to New York, I'll buy you a whole bottle, if you like," said Corporal Cuckoo, squinting as if his eyes hurt and running his fingers along the awful crevasse of that scar in his head.

I said: "That was a nasty one you got, up there."

"What? *This?*" he said, carelessly striking the scar with the flat of a hard hand. "This? Nasty one? I'll say it was a nasty one. Why, some of my brains came out. And look here—" He unbuttoned his shirt and pulled up his singlet with his left hand, while he opened and lit a battered Zippo with his right. "Take a look at that."

I cried out in astonishment. I had never seen a living body so incredibly mauled and mutilated. In the vacillating light of the flame I saw black shadows bobbing and weaving in a sort of blasted wilderness of crags, chasms, canyons, and pits. His torso was like a place laid waste by the wrath of God—burst asunder from below, scorched from above, shattered by thunderbolts, crushed by land-slides, ravaged by hurricanes. Most of his ribs, on the left-hand side, must have been smashed into fragments no bigger than the last joint of a finger by some tremendously heavy object. The bones, miraculously, had knit together again, so that there was a circle of hard bony knobs rimming a deep indentation; in that light it reminded me of one of the dead volcanos on the moon. Just under the sternum there was a dark hole, nearly three inches long, about half an inch wide, and hideously deep. I have seen such scars in the big muscles of a man's thigh—but never in the region of the breastbone. "Good God, man, you must have been torn in two and put together again!" I said. Corporal Cuckoo merely laughed, and held his lighter so that I could see his body from stomach to hips. Between the strong muscles, just under the liver, there was an old scar into which, old and healed as it was, you might have laid three fingers. Cutting across this, another scar, more than half as deep but more than twelve inches long, curved away downwards towards the groin on the left. Another appalling scar came up from somewhere below the buckle of his belt and ended in a deep triangular hole in the region of the diaphragm. And there were other scars—but the lighter went out, and Corporal Cuckoo buttoned up his shirt.

"Is that something?" he asked.

"Is that something!" I cried. "Why, good God, I'm no medical man, but I can see that the least of those wounds you've got down there ought to be enough to kill any man. How do you manage to be alive, Cuckoo? How is it possible?"

"You think you've seen something? Listen, you've seen nothing till you see my back. But never mind about that now."

"Tell me," I said, "how the devil did you come by all that? They're old scars. You couldn't have got them in this war—"

He slid down the knot of his tie, unbuttoned his collar, pulled his shirt aside, and said, dispassionately: "No. Look—this is all I got this time." He pointed nonchalantly to his throat. I counted five bullet scars in a cluster, spaced like fingertips of a half-opened hand, at the base of the throat. "Light machine-gun," he said.

"But this is impossible!" I said, while he readjusted his tie. "That little packet there must have cut one or two big arteries and smashed your spine to smithereens."

"Sure it did," said Corporal Cuckoo.

"And how old did you say you were?" I asked.

Corporal Cuckoo replied: "Round about four hundred and thirty-eight."

"Thirty-eight?"

"I said, four hundred and thirty-eight."

The man is mad, I thought. "Born 1907?" I asked.

"1507," said Corporal Cuckoo, fingering the dent in his skull. Then he went on, half-dreamily. How am I to describe his manner? It was repulsively compounded of thick stupidity, low cunning, anxiety, suspicion, and sordid calculation—it made me remember a certain peasant who tried to sell me an American wristwatch near Saint Jacques in 1944. But Corporal Cuckoo talked American, at first leering at me in the dim light, and feeling his shirt as if to assure himself that all his scars were safely buttoned away. He said, slowly: "Look . . . I'll give you the outline. It's no use you trying to sell the outline, see? You're a newspaper man. Though you might know what the whole story would be worth, there's no use you trying to sell what I'm giving you now, because you haven't got a hope in hell. But I've got to get back to work, see? I want some dough."

I said: "For roses, chickens, bees, and turpentine?"

He hesitated, and then said: "Well, yes," and rubbed his head again.

"Does it bother you?" I asked.

"Not if I don't touch that stuff you gave me," he replied, dreamily resentful.

"Where did you get that scar?" I asked.

"Battle of Turin," he said.

"I don't remember any Battle of Turin, Corporal Cuckoo. When was that?"

"Why, *the* Battle of Turin. I got this in the Pass of Suze."

"You were wounded in the Pass of Suze at the Battle of Turin, is that right? When was that?" I asked.

"1536 or 1537. King François sent us up against the Marquess de Guast. The enemy was holding the pass, but we broke through. That was my first smell of gunpowder."

"You were there of course, Corporal Cuckoo."

"Sure I was there. But I wasn't a corporal then, and my name was not Cuckoo. They called me Le Cocu. My real name was Lecoq. I came from Yvetot. I used to work for a man that made linen—Nicholas, the . . ."

Two or three minutes passed, while the Corporal told me what he thought of Nicholas. Then, having come down curse by curse out of a red cloud of passion, he continued:

". . . To cut it short Denise ran off, and all the kids in the town were singing:

Lecoq, lecoq, lecoq,
Lecoq, lecoq, lecoq . . .

I got the hell out of it and joined the army. . . . I'm not giving you anything you can make anything of, see? This is the layout, see? . . . Okay. I was about thirty, then, and in pretty good shape. Well, so when King François sent us to Turin—Monsieur de Montegan was Colonel-General of Infantry—my commander, Captain Le Rat, led us up a hill to a position, and we sure had a hot five minutes! It was anybody's battle until the rest cut through, and then we advanced, and I got *this*."

The corporal touched his head. I asked: "How?"

"From a halberdier. You know what a halberd is, don't you? It's a sort of heavy axe on the end of a ten-foot pole. You can split a man down to the waist with a halberd, if you know how to handle it. See? If it had landed straight . . . well, I guess I wouldn't be here right now. But I saw it coming, see, and I ducked, and just as I ducked my foot slipped in some blood, and I fell sideways. But all the same that halberdier got me. Right here, just where the scar is. See? Then everything went sort of black-and-white, and black, and I passed out. But I wasn't dead, see? I woke up, and there was the army doctor, with a cheap steel breastplate on—no helmet—soaked with blood up to the elbows. *Our* blood, you can bet your life—you know what medical officers are?"

I said soothingly: "Oh yes. I know, I know. And this, you say, was in 1537?"

"In 1536 or 7. I don't remember exactly. As I was saying, I woke up, and I saw the doctor, and he was talking to some other doctor that I couldn't see, and all around men were shouting their heads off—asking their friends to cut their throats and put them out of their misery . . . asking for priests . . . I thought I was in hell. My head was split wide open, and I could feel a sort of draft playing through my brains, and everything was going *bump-bump, bumpety-bump, bump-bump-bump*. But although I couldn't move or speak I could see and hear what was going on. The doctor looked at me and said . . ."

Corporal Cuckoo paused. "He said?" I asked, gently.

"Well," said Corporal Cuckoo, with scorn. "You don't even know the meaning of what you were reading in your little book— *Pipeur ou hasardeur de dez*, and all that—even when it's put down in cold print. I'll put it so that you'll understand. The doctor said something like this: 'Come here and look, sir, come and see! This fellow's brains were bursting out of his head. If I had applied theriac, he would be buried and forgotten by now. Instead, having no theriac, for want of something better, I applied my digestive. And see what has happened. His eyes have opened! Observe, also, that the bones are creeping together, and over this beating brain a sort of skin is forming. My treatment must be right, because God is healing him!' Then the one I couldn't see said something like: 'Don't be a fool, Ambroise. You're wasting your time and your medicine on a corpse.' Well, the doctor looked down at me, and touched my eyes with the ends of his fingers . . . like this . . . and I blinked. But the one I couldn't see said: 'Must you waste time and medicine on the dead?'

"After I blinked my eyes, I couldn't open them again. I couldn't see. But I could still hear, and when I heard that I was as scared as hell they were going to bury me alive. And I couldn't move. But the doctor I'd seen said: 'After five days this poor soldier's flesh is still sweet, and, weary as I am, I have my wits about me, and I swear to you that I saw his eyes open.' Then he called out: 'Jehan! Bring the digestive! . . . By your leave, sir, I will keep this man, until he comes back to life, or begins to stink. And into this wound I am going to pour some more of my digestive.'

"Then I felt something running into my head. It hurt like hell. It was like ice water dripped into your brains. I thought *This is it!*—and then I went numb all over, and then I went dead again, until I woke up later in another place. The young doctor was there, without his armor this time, but he had a sort of soft hat on. This time I could move and talk, and I asked for something to drink. When he heard me talk, the doctor opened his mouth to let out a shout, but stopped himself, and gave me some wine out of a cup. But his hands were shaking so that I got more wine in my beard than in my mouth. I used to wear a beard in those days, just like you—only a bigger one, all over my face. I heard somebody come running from the other end of the room. I saw a boy—maybe fifteen or sixteen years old. This kid opened his mouth and started to say something, but the doctor got him by the throat and said . . . put it like this: 'For your life, Jehan, be quiet!'

"The kid said: 'Master! You have brought him back from the dead!'

"Then the doctor said: 'Silence, for your life, or do you want to smell burning faggots?'

"Then I went to sleep again, and when I woke up I was in a little room, with all the windows shut, and a big fire burning so that it was hotter than hell. The doctor was there, and his name was Ambroise Paré. Maybe you have read about Ambroise Paré?"

"Do you mean the Ambroise Paré who became an army surgeon under Anne de Montmorency in the army of Francis I?"

Corporal Cuckoo said: "That's what I was saying, wasn't it? François Premier, Francis I de Montmorency was our Lieutenant-General, when we got mixed up with Charles V. The whole thing started between France and Italy, and that is how I came to get my head cracked when we went down the hill near Turin. I told you, didn't I?"

"Corporal Cuckoo," I said, "you have told me that you are four hundred and thirty-eight years old. You were born in 1507, and left Yvetot to join the army after your wife made a fool of you with a linen merchant named Nicholas. Your name was Lecoq, and the children called you 'Le Cocu.' You fought at the Battle of Turin, and were wounded in the Pass of Suze about 1537. Your head was cut open with a halberd, or pole-axe, and your brains came out. A surgeon named Ambroise Paré poured into the wound in your head what you call a digestive. So you came back to life—more than four hundred years ago! Is this right?"

"You've got it," said Corporal Cuckoo, nodding. "I knew you'd get it."

I was stupefied by the preposterousness of it all, and could only say, with what must have been a silly giggle: "Well, my venerable friend, by all accounts, after four hundred and thirty odd years of life you ought to be tremendously wise—as full of wisdom, learning, and experience as the British Museum Library."

"Why?" asked Corporal Cuckoo.

"Why? Well," I said, "it's an old story. A philosopher, let us say, or a scientist, doesn't really begin to learn anything until his life is almost ended. What wouldn't he give for five hundred extra years of life? For five hundred years of life he'd sell his soul, because given that much time, knowledge being power, he could be master of the whole world."

Corporal Cuckoo said: "Baloney! You can take it from me, bub, because I know, see? What you say might go for philosophers, and all that. They'd just go on doing what they were interested in, and they might . . . well, learn how to turn iron into gold, or something. But what about, well, for instance a baseball player, or a boxer. What would they do with five hundred years? What they were fit to do—swing bats or throw leather! What would *you* do?"

"Why, of course, you're right, Corporal Cuckoo," I said. "I'd just go on and on banging on a typewriter and chucking my money down the drain, so that in five hundred years from now I'd be no wiser and no richer than I am at this moment."

"No, wait a minute," he said, tapping my arm with a finger that felt like a rod of iron, and leering at me shrewdly. "You'd go on writing books and things. You're paid on a percentage basis, so in five hundred years you'd have more than you could spend. But how about me? All I'm fit for is to be in the army. I don't give a damn for philosophy, and all that stuff. It don't mean a thing to me. I'm no wiser now than I was when I was thirty. I never did go in for reading, and all that stuff, and I never will. My ambition is to get me a place like Jack Dempsey's on Broadway."

"I thought you said you wanted to grow roses, and chickens, and bees, and turpentine trees, and whatnot," I said.

"Yeah, that's right."

"How do you reconcile the two? . . . I mean, how does a restaurant on Broadway fit in with bees and roses, etcetera?"

"Well, it's like this . . ." said Corporal Cuckoo.

". . . I told you about how Doctor Paré healed up my head when it was split open so that my brains were coming out. Well, after I could walk about a bit he let me stay in his house, and I can tell you, he fed me on the fat of the land, though he didn't live any too damn well himself. Yeahp, he looked after me like a son—a hell of a lot better than my old man ever looked after me . . . chickens, eggs in wine, anything I wanted. If I said 'I guess I'd like a pie made with skylarks for dinner,' I had it. If I said: 'Doc, this wine is kind of sour,' up came a bottle of Alicante, or something. Inside two or three weeks, I was fitter and stronger than I'd ever been before. So then I got kind of restless and said I wanted to go. Well, Doctor Paré said he wanted me to stay. I said to him: 'I'm an active man, Doc, and I've got my living to get; and before I got this little crack on the head I heard that there was money to be made in one army or another right now.'

"Well, then Doctor Paré offered me a couple of pieces of gold to stay in his house for another month. I took the money, but I knew then that he was up to something, and I went out of my way to find out. I mean, he was an army surgeon, and I was nothing but a lousy infantryman. There was a catch in it somewhere, see? So I acted dumb, but I kept my eyes open, and made friends with Jehan, the kid that helped around the doctor's office. This Jehan was a big-eyed, skinny kid, with one leg a bit shorter than the other, and he thought I was a hell of a fellow when I cracked a walnut between two fingers, and lifted up the big table, that must have weighed about five hundred pounds, on my back. This Jehan, he told me he'd always wanted to be a powerful guy like me. But he'd been sick since before he was born, and might not have lived at all if Doctor Paré hadn't saved his life. Well, so I went to work on Jehan, and I found out what the doctor's game was. You know doctors, eh?"

Corporal Cuckoo nudged me, and I said: "Uhuh, go on."

"Well it seems that up to the time when we got through the Pass of Suze, they'd treated what they called 'poisoned wounds' with boiling oil of elder with a dash of what they called theriac. Theriac was nothing much more than honey and herbs. Well, so it seems that by the time we went up the hill, Doctor Paré had run out of the oil of elder and theriac, and so, for want of something better, he mixed up what he called a digestive.

"My commander, Captain Le Rat, the one that got the bullet that smashed up his ankle, was the first one to be dosed with digestive. His ankle got better," said Corporal Cuckoo, snapping his fingers, "—like *that*. I was the third or fourth soldier to get a dose of Doctor Paré's digestive. The Doc was looking over the battlefield, because he wanted a dead body to cut up on the side. You know how doctors are. This kid Jehan told me he wanted a brain to play around with. Well, there I was, see, with my brains showing. All the doctor had to do was reach down and help himself. Well, to cut it short, he saw that I was breathing, and wondered how the hell a man could be breathing after he'd got what I had. So he poured some of his digestive into the hole in my head, tied it up, and watched for developments. I told you what happened then. I came back to life. More than that, the bones in my head grew together. Doctor Ambroise Paré believed he'd got something. So he was keeping me sort of under observation, and making notes.

"I know doctors. Well, anyway, I went to work on Jehan. I said: 'Be a good fellow, Jehan, tell a pal what *is* this digestive, or whatever your master calls it?'

"Jehan said: 'Why, sir, my master makes no secret of it. It is nothing but a mixture of egg yolks, oil of roses and turpentine.' (I don't mind telling you that, bub, because it's already been printed.)"

I said to Corporal Cuckoo; "I don't know how the devil you come by these curious facts, but I happen to know that they're true. They are available in several histories of medicine. Ambroise Paré's digestive, with which he treated the wounded after the Battle of Turin was, as you say, nothing but a mixture of oil of roses, egg yolks, and turpentine. And it is also a fact that the first wounded man upon whom he tried it really was Captain Le Rat, in 1537. Paré said at the time: 'I dressed his wounds and God healed him' . . . Well?"

"Yeahp," said Corporal Cuckoo, with a sneer. "Sure. Turpentine, oil of roses, eggs. That's right. You know the proportions?"

"No, I don't," I said.

"I know you don't, bub. Well, I do. See? And I'll tell you some-thing else. It's not just oil of roses, eggs, and turpentine—there was one other thing Doc Paré slipped in in my case, for an experi-ment—see? And I know what it is."

I said: "Well, go on."

"Well, I could see that this Doctor Ambroise Paré was going to make something out of me, see? So I kept my eyes open, and I waited, and I worked on Jehan, until I found out just where the doctor kept his notebook. I mean, in those days you could get sixty or seventy thousand dollars for a bit of bone they called a 'uni-corn's horn.' Hell, I mean, if I had something that could just about bring a man back from the dead—draw his bones together and put him on his feet in a week or two, even if his brains were coming out—hell, everybody was having a war then, and I could have been rich in a few minutes."

I said: "No doubt about that. What—"

"—What the hell," said Corporal Cuckoo. "What the hell right did he have to use me for a guinea pig? Where would he have been if it hadn't been for me? And where do you think I'd have been after? Out on my neck with two or three gold pieces, while the doctor grabbed the credit and made millions out of it. I wanted to open a place in Paris—girls and everything, see? Could I do that on two or three gold pieces? I ask you! Okay; one night when Doctor Paré and Jehan were out, I took his notebook, slipped out of a win-dow, and got the hell out of it.

"As soon as I thought I was safe, I went into a saloon, and drank some wine, and got into conversation with a girl. It seems some-body else was interested in this girl, and there was a fight. The other guy cut me in the face with a knife. I had a knife too. You know how it is—all of a sudden I felt something pulling my knife out of my hand, and I saw that I'd pushed it between this man's ribs. He was one of those mean little guys, about a hundred and twenty pounds, with a screwed-up face. (She was a great big girl with yellow hair.) I could see that I'd killed him, so I ran for my life, and I left my knife where it was—stuck tight between his ribs.

I hid out, expecting trouble. But they never found me. Most of that night I lay under a hedge. I was pretty sick. I mean, he'd cut me from just under the eye to the back of my head—and cut me deep. He'd cut the top of my right ear off, clean. It wasn't only that it hurt like hell, but I knew I could be identified by that cut. I'd left half an ear behind me. It was me for the gallows, see? So I kept as quiet as I could, in a ditch, and went to sleep for a few hours before dawn. And then, when I woke up, that cut didn't hurt at all, not even my ear—and I can tell you that a cut ear sure does hurt. I went and washed my face in a pond, and when the water got still enough so I could see myself, I saw that that cut and this ear had healed right up so that the marks looked five years old. All that in half a night! So I went on my way. About two days later, a farmer's dog bit me in the leg—took a piece out. Well, a bite like that ought to take weeks to heal up. But mine didn't. It was all healed over by next day, and there was hardly a scar. That stuff Paré poured into my head had made me so that any wound I might get, anywhere, anytime, would just heal right up—like magic. I knew I had something when I grabbed those papers of Paré's. But this was terrific!"

"You had them still, Corporal Cuckoo?"

"What do you think? Sure I had them, wrapped up in a bit of linen and tied round my waist—four pieces of . . . not paper, the other stuff, parchment. That's it, parchment. Folded across, and sewn up along the fold. The outside bit was blank, like a cover. But the six pages inside were all written over. The hell of it was, I couldn't read. I'd never been learned. See? Well, I had the best part of my two gold pieces left, and I pushed on to Paris."

I asked: "Didn't Ambroise Paré say anything?"

Corporal Cuckoo sneered again. "What the hell could he say?" he asked. "Say what? Say he'd resurrected the dead with his digestive? That would have finished him for sure. Where was his evidence? And you can bet your life that kid Jehan kept *his* mouth shut: he wouldn't want the doctor to know he'd squealed. See? No, nobody said a word. I got into Paris okay."

"What did you do there?" I asked.

"My idea was to find somebody I could trust, to read those

papers for me, see? If you want to know how I got my living, well, I did the best I could . . . never mind what. Well, one night, in a place where I was, I came across a student, mooching drinks, an educated man with no place to sleep. I showed him the doctor's papers, and asked him what they meant. They made him think a bit, but he got the hang of them. The doctor had written down just how he'd mixed that digestive of his, and that only filled up one page. Four of the other pages were full of figures, and the only other writing was on the last page. It was all about me. And how he'd cured me."

I said: "With the yolks of eggs, oil of roses, and turpentine?"

Corporal Cuckoo nodded, and said: "Yeahp. Them three and something else."

I said: "I'll bet you anything you like I know what the fourth ingredient is, in this digestive."

"What'll you bet?" asked Corporal Cuckoo.

I said: "I'll bet you a beehive."

"What do you mean?"

"Why, Corporal, it stands to reason. You said you wanted to raise chickens, roses, and bees. You said you wanted to go south for turpentine. You accounted for egg yolks, oil of roses, and turpentine in Doctor Paré's formula. What would a man like you want with bees? Obviously the fourth ingredient is honey."

"Yeahp," said Corporal Cuckoo. "You're right, bub. The doctor slipped in some honey. . . ." He opened a jackknife, looked at me narrowly, then snapped the blade back again and pocketed the knife, saying: "You don't know the proportions. You don't know how to mix the stuff. You don't know how hot it ought to be, or how slow you've got to let it cool."

"So you have the secret of life?" I said. "You're four hundred years old, and wounds can't kill you. It only takes a certain mixture of egg yolks, oil of roses, turpentine and honey. . . . Is that right?"

"That's right," said Corporal Cuckoo.

"Well, didn't you think of buying the ingredients and mixing them yourself?"

"Well, yes, I did. The doctor had said in his notes how the digestive he'd given me and Captain Le Rat had been kept in a bottle in the dark for two years. So I made a wine bottle full of the stuff and kept it covered up away from the light for two years, wherever I went. Then me and some friends of mine got into a bit of trouble, and one of my friends, a guy called Pierre Solitude got a pistol bullet in the chest. I tried the stuff on him, but he died. At the same time I got a sword-thrust in the side. Believe me or not, that healed up in nine hours, inside and out, of its own accord. You can make what you like of that. . . . It all came out of something to do with robbing a church.

"I got out of France, and lived as best I could for about a year until I found myself in Salzburg. That was about four years after the battle in the Pass of Suze. Well, in Salzburg I came across some guy who told me that the greatest doctor in the world was in town. I remember that doctor's name, because, well, who wouldn't? It was Aureolus Theophrastus Bombastus von Hohenheim. He'd been a big shot in Basle a few years before. He was otherwise known as Paracelsus. He wasn't doing much then.' He hung around, most of the time, drinking himself crazy in a wine cellar called The Three Doves. I met him there one night—it must have been in 1541—and said my piece when nobody else was listening." Corporal Cuckoo laughed harshly.

I said: "Paracelsus was a very great man. He was one of the great doctors of the world."

"Oh, hell, he was only a fat old drunk. Certainly was higher than a kite when I saw him. Yelling his head off, banging on the table with an empty can. When I told him about this stuff, in strict confidence, he got madder than ever, called me everything he could think of—and believe me, he could think of plenty—and bent the can over my head. Broke the skin just where the hair starts. I was going to take a poke at him, but then he calmed down a bit and said in Swiss-German, I think it was, 'Experiment, experiment! A demonstration! A demonstration! If you come back tomorrow and show me that cut perfectly healed, charlatan, I'll listen to you.' Then he burst out laughing, and I thought to myself, I'll give you something to laugh at, bub. So I took a walk, and that little cut healed up and was gone inside the hour. Then I went back to show him. I'd sort of taken a liking to the old soak, see? Well, when I get back to this tavern there's Doctor von Hohenheim, or Paracelsus, if you like, lying on his back dying of a dagger stab. He'd gotten into a fight with a woodcarver, and this woodcarver was as soused as he was, see? And so he let this Paracelsus have it. I never did have no luck, and I never will. We might have got along together, me and him: I only talked to him for half an hour, but so help me, you knew who was the boss when he was there, alright! Oh well, that was that."

"And then?" I asked.

"I'm just giving you the outline, see? If you want the whole story it's going to cost you plenty," said Corporal Cuckoo. "I bummed around Salzburg for a year, got whipped out of town for being a beggar, got the hell out of it to Switzerland, and signed on with a bunch of paid soldiers, what they called *condottieri*, under a Swiss colonel, and did a bit of fighting in Italy. There was supposed to be good pickings there. But somebody stole my little bit of loot, and we never even got half our pay in the end. Then I went to France, and met a sea captain by the name of Bordelais who was carrying brandy to England and was short of a man. A fast little English pirate boat stopped us in the Channel, and grabbed the cargo, cut Bordelais' throat and slung the crew overboard—all except me. The limey captain, Hawker, liked the look of me. I joined the crew, but I never was much of a sailor. That hooker—hell, she wasn't bigger than one of the lifeboats on this ship—was called the *Harry*, after the King of England, Henry VIII, the one they made a movie about. Still, we did alright. We specialized in French brandy: stopped the froggy boats in mid-channel, grabbed the cargo, shoved the captain and crew overboard. 'Dead men tell no tales,' old Hawker always said. Well, I jumped the ship somewhere near Romney, with money in my pocket—I didn't like the sea, see? I'd had half a dozen nasty wounds, but they couldn't kill me. I was worried about what'd happen if I went overboard. You could shoot me through the head and not kill me, though it'd hurt like hell for a few days while the wound healed itself. But I just hated to think of what would happen if somebody tried to drown me. Get it? I'd have to wait under water till the fishes ate me, or till I just sort of naturally rotted away—alive all the time. And that's not nice.

"Well, as I was saying, I quit at Romney and got to London. There was an oldish widow with a linen-draper's business near London Bridge. She had a bit of dough, and she took a fancy to me. Well, what the hell? I got married to her. Lived with her about thirteen years. She was a holy terror, at first, but I corrected her. Her name was Rose, and she died just about when Queen Elizabeth got to be queen of England. That was around 1558, I guess. She was scared of me—Rose, I mean, not Queen Elizabeth, because I was always playing around with honey, and eggs, and turpentine, and oil of roses. She got older and older, and I stayed exactly the same as I was when I married her, and she didn't like that one little bit. She thought I was a witch. Said I had the philosophers' stone, and knew the secret of perpetual youth. Hah, so help me, she wasn't so damn far wrong. She wanted me to let her in on it. But, as I was saying, I kept working on those notes of Doctor Paré's, and I mixed honey, turpentine, oil of roses, and yolks of eggs, just as he'd done, in the right proportions, at the proper temperature, and kept the mixture bottled in the dark for the right length of time . . . and still it didn't work."

I asked Corporal Cuckoo: "How did you find out that your mixture didn't work?"

"Well, I tried it on Rose. She kept at me until I did. Every now and again we had kind of a lovers' quarrel, and I tried the digestive on her afterwards. But she took as long to heal as any ordinary person would have taken. The interesting thing was, that I not only couldn't be killed by a wound—*I couldn't get any older! I couldn't catch any diseases! I couldn't die!* And you can figure this for yourself—if some stuff that cured any sort of wound was worth a fortune, what would it be worth to me if I had something that would make people stay young and healthy forever? Eh?" He paused.

I said: "Interesting speculation. You might have given some of the stuff, for example, to Shakespeare. *He* got better and better as he went on. I wonder what he would have arrived at by now? I don't know, though. If Shakespeare had swallowed an elixir of life and perpetual youth when he was very young, he would have remained as he was; young and undeveloped. Maybe he might still be holding horses outside theatres . . . or whistling for taxis, a stage-struck country boy of undeveloped genius. If, on the other hand, he had taken the stuff when he wrote, say, *The Tempest*—there he'd be still, burnt up, worn out, world-weary, tied to death and unable to die. . . . On the other hand, of course, some debauched rake of the Elizabethan period could go on being a debauched rake at high pressure, for centuries and centuries. But, oh my God, how bored he would get after a hundred years or so, and how he'd long for death! That would be dangerous stuff, that stuff of yours, Corporal Cuckoo!"

"Shakespeare?" he said, "Shakespeare? William Shakespeare. I met him. I met a buddy of his when I was fighting in the Netherlands, and he introduced us when we got back to London. William Shakespeare—puffy-faced man, bald on top; used to wave his hands about when he talked. He took an interest in me. We talked a whole lot together."

"What did he say?" I asked.

Corporal Cuckoo replied: "Oh, hell, how am I to remember every god damn word? He just asked questions, the same as you do. We just talked."

"And how did he strike you?" I asked.

Corporal Cuckoo considered, and then said, slowly: "The kind of man that counts his change and leaves a nickel tip . . . one of these days I'm going to read his books, but I've never had much time for reading."

I said: "So, I take it that your only interest in Paré's digestive has been a financial interest. You merely wanted to make money out of it. Is that so?"

"Why, sure," said Corporal Cuckoo, "I've had *my* shot of the stuff. *I'm alright.*"

"Corporal Cuckoo, has it occurred to you that what you are after is next door to impossible?"

"How's that?"

"Well," I said, "your Paré's digestive is made of egg yolk, oil of roses, turpentine, and honey. Isn't that so?"

"Well, yes. So what? What's impossible about that?"

I said: "You know how a chicken's diet alters the taste of an egg, don't you?"

"Well?"

"What a chicken eats changes not only the taste, but the color of an egg. Any chicken farmer can tell you that. Isn't that so?"

"Well?"

"Well, what a chicken eats goes into the egg, doesn't it—just as the fodder that you feed a cow comes out in the milk? Have you stopped to consider how many different sorts of chickens there have been in the world since the Battle of Turin in 1537, and the varieties of chicken feed they might have pecked up in order to lay their eggs? Have you thought that the egg yolk is only one of four ingredients mixed in Ambroise Paré's digestive. Is it possible that it has not occurred to you that this one ingredient involves permutations and combinations of several millions of other ingredients?"

Corporal Cuckoo was silent. I went on: "Then take the roses. If no two eggs are exactly alike, what about roses? You come from a wine-growing country, you say! Then you must know that the mere thickness of a wall can separate two entirely different kinds of wine—that a noble vintage may be crushed out of grapes grown less than two feet away from a vine that is good for nothing. The same applies to tobacco. Have you stopped to think of your roses? Roses are pollinated by bees, bees go from flower to flower, making them fertile. Your oil of roses, therefore, embodies an infinity of possible ingredients. Does it not?"

Corporal Cuckoo was still silent. I continued, with a kind of malicious enthusiasm. "You must reflect on these things, Corporal. Take turpentine. It comes out of trees. Even in the sixteenth century there were many known varieties of turpentine—Chian terebinthine, and what not. But above all, my dear fellow, consider honey! There are more kinds of honey in the world than have ever been categorized. Every honeycomb yields a slightly different honey. You must know that bees living in heather gather and store one kind of honey, while bees in an apple orchard give us something quite different. It is all honey, of course, but its flavor and quality is variable beyond calculation. Honey varies from hive to hive, Corporal Cuckoo. I say nothing of wild bees' honey."

"Well?" he said, glumly.

"Well. All this is relatively simple, Corporal, in relation to what comes next. I don't know how many beehives there are in the world. Assume that in every hive there are—let us be moderate—one thousand bees. (There are more than that, of course, but I am trying to simplify.) You must realize that every one of these bees brings home a slightly different drop of honey. Every one of these bees may, in her travels, take honey from fifty different flowers. The honey accumulated by all the bees in the hive is mixed together. Any single cell in any honeycomb out of any hive contains scores of subtly different elements! I say nothing of the time element; honey six months old is very different from honey out of the same hive, left for ten years. From day to day, honey changes. Now taking all possible combinations of eggs, roses, turpentine and honey . . . where are you? Answer me that, Corporal Cuckoo."

Corporal Cuckoo struggled with this for a few seconds, and then said: "I don't get it. You think I'm nuts, don't you?"

"I never said so," I said, uneasily.

"No, you never *said* so. Well, listen. Don't give me all that double talk. I'm doing you a favor. Look—"

He took out and opened his jackknife, and scrutinized his left hand, looking for an unscarred area of skin. "No!" I shouted, and gripped his knife-hand. I might have been trying to hold back the piston rod of a great locomotive. My grip and my weight were nothing to Corporal Cuckoo's.

"—Look," he said, calmly, and cut through the soft flesh between the thumb and forefinger of his left hand until the knife-blade stopped on the bone, and the thumb fell back until it touched the forearm. "See that?"

I saw it through a mist. The great ship seemed, suddenly, to roll and plunge. "Are you crazy?" I said, as soon as I could.

"No," said Corporal Cuckoo. "I'm showing you I'm not, see?" He held out his mutilated hand close to my face.

"Take it away," I said.

"Sure," said Corporal Cuckoo. "Watch this." He pushed the almost-severed thumb back into place, and held it down with his right hand. "It's okay," he said, "there's no need to look sick. I'm showing you, see? Don't go—sit down. I'm not kidding. I can give you a hell of a story, a fact story. I can show you Paré's little note-book and everything. You saw what I showed you when I pulled up my shirt? You saw what I've got right here, on the left side?"

I said: "Yes."

"Well, that's where I got hit by a nine-pound cannon ball when I was on the *Mary Ambree*, fighting against the Spanish Armada—it smashed my chest so that the ribs went through my heart—and I was walking about in two weeks. And this other one on the right, under the ribs—tomorrow I'll show you what it looks like from the back—I got that one at the Battle of Fontenoy; and there's a hell of a good story there. A French cannon ball came down and hit a broken sword that a dead officer had dropped, and it sent that sword flying right through me, lungs and liver and all. So help me, it came out through my right shoulder blade. The other one lower down was a bit of a bombshell at the Battle of Waterloo—I was opened up like a pig—it wasn't worth the surgeon's while to do anything about it. But I was on my feet in six days, while men with broken legs were dying like flies. I can prove it, I tell you! And listen—I marched to Quebec with Benedict Arnold. Sit still and listen—my right leg was smashed to pulp all the way down from the hip to the ankle at Balaklava. It knitted together before the sur-geon had a chance to get around to me—he couldn't believe his eyes, he thought he was dreaming. I can tell you a hell of a story! But it's worth dough, see? Now, this is my proposition—I'll tell it, you write it, and we'll split fifty-fifty, and I'll start my farm. What d'you say?"

I heard myself saying, in a sickly, stupid voice: "Why didn't you save some of your pay, all those years?"

Corporal Cuckoo replied, with scorn: "Why didn't I save my

pay! Because I'm what I *am*, you mug! Hell, once upon a time, if I'd kept away from cards, I could've bought Manhattan Island for less than what I lost to a Dutchman called Bruncker drawing ace-high for English guineas! Save my pay! If it wasn't one thing it was another. I lay off liquor. Okay. So if it's not liquor, it's a woman. I lay off women. Okay. Then it's cards or dice. I always *meant* to save my pay; but I never had it *in* me to save my goddam pay! Doctor Paré's stuff fixed me—and when I say it fixed me, I mean, it fixed me, just like I was, and am, and always will be. See? A foot soldier, ignorant as dirt. It took me nearly a hundred years to learn to write my name, and four hundred years to get to be a corporal. How d'you like that? And it took will power, at that! Now here's my proposition: fifty-fifty on the story. Once I get proper publicity in a magazine, I'll be able to let the digestive out of my hands with an easy mind—see? Because nobody'd dare to try any funny business with a man with nationwide publicity. Eh?"

"No, of course not," I said.

"Eh?"

"Sure, sure, Corporal."

"Good," said Corporal Cuckoo. "Now in case you think I'm kidding, take a look at this. You saw what I done?"

"I saw, Corporal."

"Look," he said, thrusting his left hand under my nose. It was covered with blood. His shirt-cuff was red and wet. Fascinated, I saw one thick, sluggish drop crawl out of the cloth near the buttonhole and hang, quivering, before it fell on my knee. The mark of it is in the cloth of my trousers to this day.

"See?" said Corporal Cuckoo, and he licked the place between his fingers where his knife had cut down. A pale area appeared. "Where did I cut myself?" he asked.

I shook my head: there was no wound—only a white scar. He wiped his knife on the palm of his hand—it left a red smear—and let the blade fall with a sharp click. Then he wiped his left hand on his right, rubbed both hands clean upon the backs of his trouser legs, and said, "Am I kidding?"

"Well!" I said, somewhat breathlessly. "Well . . . !"

"Oh, what the hell!" groaned Corporal Cuckoo, weary beyond words, exhausted, worn out by his endeavors to explain the inexplicable and make the incredible sound reasonable. ". . . Look. You think this is a trick? Have you got a knife?"

"Yes. Why?"

"A big knife?"

"Moderately big."

"Okay. Cut my throat with it, and see what happens. Stick it in me wherever you like. And I'll bet you a thousand dollars I'll be alright inside two or three hours. . . . Go on. Man to man, it's a bet. Or go borrow an axe if you like; hit me over the head with it."

"Be damned if I do," I said, shuddering.

"And that's how it is," said Corporal Cuckoo, in despair. "And that's how it is every time. There they are, making fortunes out of soap and toothpaste . . . and here I am, with something in my pocket to keep you young and healthy forever—ah, go and chase yourself! I never ought to've drunk your rotten Scotch. This is the way it always is. You wear a beard just like I used to wear before I got a gunpowder burn in the chin at Zutphen, when Sir Philip Sidney got his; or I wouldn't have talked to you. Oh, you dope! I could murder you, so help me I could! Go to hell!"

Corporal Cuckoo leapt to his feet and darted away so swiftly that before I found my feet he had disappeared. There was blood on the deck close to where I had been sitting—a tiny pool of blood, no larger than a coffee-saucer, broken at one edge by the imprint of a heel. About a yard and a half away I saw another heel mark in blood, considerably less noticeable. Then there was a dull smear, as if one of the bloody rubber heels had spun around and impelled its owner towards the left. "Cuckoo! Cuckoo!" I shouted. "Oh, Cuckoo! Cuckoo!"

But I never saw Corporal Cuckoo again, and I wonder where he can be. It may be that he gave me a false name. But what I heard I heard, and what I saw I saw; and I have five hundred dollars here in an envelope for the man who will put me in touch with him. Honey and oil of roses, eggs and turpentine; these involve, as I said, infinite permutations and combinations. So does any comparable mixture. Still, it might be worth investigating. Why not? Fleming got penicillin out of mildew. Only God knows the glorious mysteries of the dust, out of which come trees and bees and life in every form, from mildew to man.

I lost Corporal Cuckoo before we landed in New York on July 11, 1945. Somewhere in the United States, I believe, there is a man, tremendously strong in the arms, and covered with terrible scars, who has the dreadfully dangerous secret of perpetual youth and life. He appears to be about thirty-odd years of age, and has watery, greenish eyes.

NEW & FORTHCOMING TITLES FROM VALANCOURT BOOKS

R. C. Ashby (Ruby Ferguson)	He Arrived at Dusk
Frank Baker	The Birds
Walter Baxter	Look Down in Mercy
Charles Beaumont	The Hunger and Other Stories
Paul Binding	Harmonica's Bridegroom
John Blackburn	A Scent of New-Mown Hay
	Broken Boy
	Blue Octavo
	Nothing But the Night
	Bury Him Darkly
	The Household Traitors
	Our Lady of Pain
	A Beastly Business
Thomas Blackburn	The Feast of the Wolf
John Braine	Room at the Top
	The Vodi
Basil Copper	The Great White Space
	Necropolis
Ronald Fraser	Flower Phantoms
Stephen Gilbert	The Burnaby Experiments
Claude Houghton	I Am Jonathan Scrivener
	This Was Ivor Trent
Gerald Kersh	Nightshade and Damnations
Francis King	To the Dark Tower
	Never Again
	An Air that Kills
	The Dividing Stream
	The Dark Glasses
	The Man on the Rock
C.H.B. Kitchin	Ten Pollitt Place
	The Book of Life
Hilda Lewis	The Witch and the Priest
Kenneth Martin	Aubade
	Waiting for the Sky to Fall
Michael McDowell	The Amulet
Michael Nelson	Knock or Ring
	A Room in Chelsea Square

Oliver Onions	The Hand of Kornelius Voyt
Dennis Parry	Sea of Glass
Robert Phelps	Heroes and Orators
J.B. Priestley	Benighted
	The Other Place
Forrest Reid	The Garden God
	The Tom Barber Trilogy
Henry de Vere Stacpoole	The Blue Lagoon
John Trevena	Furze the Cruel
	Sleeping Waters
John Wain	Hurry on Down
	The Smaller Sky
Hugh Walpole	The Killer and the Slain
Keith Waterhouse	There is a Happy Land
	Billy Liar
Alec Waugh	The Loom of Youth
Colin Wilson	Ritual in the Dark
	The Philosopher's Stone

Selected Eighteenth and Nineteenth Century Classics

Anonymous	Teleny
	The Sins of the Cities of the Plain
Grant Allen	Miss Cayley's Adventures
Joanna Baillie	Six Gothic Dramas
Eaton Stannard Barrett	The Heroine
William Beckford	Azemia
Countess of Blessington	Marmaduke Herbert
Mary Elizabeth Braddon	Thou Art the Man
John Buchan	Sir Quixote of the Moors
Hall Caine	The Manxman
Mona Caird	The Wing of Azrael
Mary Cholmondeley	Diana Tempest
Marie Corelli	The Sorrows of Satan
	Ziska
Caroline Clive	Paul Ferroll
Baron Corvo	Stories Toto Told Me
	Hubert's Arthur
Gabriele D'Annunzio	The Intruder (L'innocente)

CPSIA information can be obtained at www.ICGtesting.com
Printed in the USA
BVOW02s0927181113

336506BV00001B/20/P